Melbourne Men

BOOKS 1 & 2

TAMSIN BAKER

Danny's Coming Out

Chapter One

MARCUS WINCED as he glanced around the room, focusing from one feminine touch to another even more tragic one. Sienna's thirtieth birthday party was being held at her parents' glorious home and she had almost managed to destroy all of its Edwardian charm in one fell swoop.

She'd gone for a pink and black theme, which, if done well, was fun and elegant. However, the fluorescent pink drinks, matching party food, and plastic fuchsia curtains were over the top, even for her.

The birthday girl herself, in a skin-tight white dress, greeted him with a huge smile, arms outstretched.

"Marcus! I'm so glad you could make it!"

Marcus grinned as she threw herself into his arms, her warm body and full breasts pressing against his chest. No woman could resist the safety of a gay man, it would seem.

"I told you I'd come. No way was I missing the big three zero!" He winked at her then grinned as she screwed up her pretty face into a grotesque grimace. Thirty was a significant milestone for most people, yet everyone he knew dreaded it. Crazy. After all, it was just a number. But not for him. He'd been proud of what he'd achieved in such a short time.

"Just because I thought thirty was old when I was twenty-one doesn't mean I still think it."

Marcus laughed aloud at that one as his mind conjured up a picture of the twenty-one-year-old Sienna in jeans so low everyone could see her bum crack. He'd known Sienna since university and she'd barely changed in appearance or personality. It was unfortunate that their group didn't get together more, but work and family always seemed to get in the way. "Personally, I think you are more beautiful than you were ten years ago. But, hey, that's just my humble opinion."

Sienna giggled away his compliment, but Marcus caught the way her cheeks flushed to match the curtains and was glad she appeared pleased by his words. She deserved to be proud of herself. She looked good enough to eat. If he'd been straight, he would have been very tempted. He reached out and touched her arm to get her attention once again.

"It was nice of your parents to host the party for you."

Sienna's lips curled into a smile. She sighed with contentment and looked around the room.

"Yeah, my apartment is way too small and they offered so..."

As Sienna finished talking, a huge man walked up, his feet sounding a loud thud on wooden floors with each step. He pulled Sienna close, slipped a hand around her waist and laid it across her flat belly.

Well, hello, possessive caveman.

"Babe, who's this?" The hulk's strong mouth turned down in disapproval.

Marcus smiled politely, waiting for his friend to make the introductions.

"Steve, this is Marcus. Remember... my friend from university? The one I told you about." Sienna made a nodding motion and her eyes widened.

Marcus suppressed the impulse to reach out and pinch her cheeky little ass. When would people learn it was rude to do that? He was gay, not a different species, for God's sake!

Realizing he wasn't a threat, the boyfriend's stiff posture relaxed, his shoulders dropped, and a soft smile picked up the corners of his mouth.

"Marcus? Oh, yeah, that's right."

A sigh arose within Marcus, but he stopped himself from behaving rudely.

Steve cleared his throat and awkwardly held out his hand, making pretty good eye contact for a hetero gorilla.

"Hey, man."

Marcus lifted his eyebrows in surprise, but he reached out and shook the Hulk's hand. Sienna had done well to find a man not as homophobic as most. *I'm impressed.*

He tilted his head toward Sienna. "Nice to meet you. You've got a great girl here."

"Yeah, I know."

Watching Steve's eyes soften as he grabbed Sienna once again, envy, sharp and hot, pulsed through him like bolts of electricity. He didn't want to be straight, he loved being who he was. But damn, he wanted *that*. Someone to look at him like Steve was looking at Sienna. Someone to stare at him the way Sienna was staring adoringly at Steve.

Soon, maybe. Hopefully.

A gorgeous young man with short blond hair walked up behind Sienna and pulled at her elbow. She turned and listened attentively while the stranger whispered in her ear.

Who's that? He's stunning! That gorgeous smooth skin and those lush lips are just begging to be kissed.

"That's perfect. Thanks, sweetie." She smiled and he disappeared out of the room once again.

Marcus's gay radar blared with the strength of a megaphone and his heart pounded a little harder within his chest. Was it possible he'd found another non-heterosexual at this party? Really?

"Who was that, Sienna?" He took a sip of his beer and glanced away. He had to use all his control not to seem overly interested in the answer.

She stood on her tiptoes and waved her hand over her head, signaling to someone behind him.

"Oh, just my baby brother. I'm sure you've met him before. Talk to you later, Marcus?" Before he could answer, she'd disappeared to fulfill her hostess duties with hunky Steve following her.

Well, he'd done his duty. He'd come, dropped off his present and said happy birthday to the birthday girl. Some of his gay friends had invited him out to a club later and he'd arranged to meet them at eleven, but did he still want to go?

Marcus stood still, tapping his fingers against his thighs, unable to decide what to do. His compulsion to stay and the strength of his curiosity shocked him. Could that gorgeous guy really be Sienna's brother? He couldn't be so unlucky as to be attracted to the only guy he shouldn't touch. Sienna would surely kill him.

He strolled over to the door that led out into the garden as butterflies fluttered within his belly and a grin surfaced. It wasn't *terrible,* he supposed, but corrupting a boy so beautiful would surely be something to put in the naughty pile.

His attention moved around the backyard, casting a professional eye over his surroundings. It was a big house, beautifully landscaped with rows of hedges, native flowers, and even a water feature. Sienna had moved out of her parents' home years ago, but it was the perfect place for a party this size. She was very lucky they were so accommodating.

Marcus took a deep breath and stepped out onto the brick-paved area. Glancing around the backyard and trying to be subtle, he looked around for her brother. It couldn't hurt, surely, just to talk to him.

He sighed and took another sip of beer. There were heterosexual couples everywhere, standing around, talking and drinking. He couldn't see anyone who looked anything like Sienna's brother. *Damn.*

Smoke tendrils floating above the hedges of the back garden caught his attention and he strode down the bricked path before he had made the conscious choice to investigate.

As he rounded the hedge, he stopped short, his gut tightening in anticipation. In the back corner of the garden was a hidden alcove with an iron garden seat poised opposite another water feature. *What a perfect place for a rendezvous.*

Sitting on the seat all by himself having a cigarette was the blond-haired, blue-eyed brother. The man caught sight of him and looked up and grinned, his eyes dancing with mirth. White teeth dazzled, even in the dim light.

"You caught me. Did my sister send you out here?"

His voice was as beautiful as he was. Rich, smooth, lovely. Marcus suppressed the need to shiver. The hairs on his neck prickled up and he shook his head. "No, I just saw puffs of smoke and thought I'd join you."

Not bad, old man. That was pretty smooth.

It had been years since Marcus had picked up a cigarette, but hell, he'd use any excuse to chat up the guy for a few minutes.

Sienna's brother seemed to be waiting for something and he realized that the blond hottie was expecting him to start smoking, so he moved closer. Figuring honesty worked best, he shrugged. "I quit years ago but still crave one when I have a beer. Can I bum one off you?" He stepped even closer and as his eyes adjusted to the dark, he took a good look at Sienna's brother.

He had her flawless skin and bright blue eyes but that was where the similarities stopped. He had a strong jaw, full lips, and tousled I-just-rolled-out-of-bed hair.

"Sure." The guy, whose name he still didn't know, held out a packet of his old brand.

He groaned, true longing flooding him like happiness at seeing an old friend. He'd kicked the habit, good and proper, but it was amazing how his body remembered the pleasure. "I miss my Winnie Blues."

He sighed and reached for the coveted item. Instead of grabbing one cigarette, he took the packet, intentionally making contact with the guy's fingers.

As Marcus made a show of drawing one out and putting it to his lips, sparks flickered in the young man's eyes.

"I'm Marcus, by the way." He handed the pack of cigarettes back.

The young man swallowed in obvious nervousness, his legs shifting restlessly as he palmed the packet and placed them on the seat next to him.

"I'm Daniel... Danny."

Danny stood up, pulled a lighter from his jeans and flicked his thumb on it. The flame shot up and Marcus moved closer, watching the way Danny's eyes widened in awareness, but he didn't pull away.

He held Danny's hand steady and drew the lighter closer to him. He tilted his head and keeping eye contact with the beautiful baby brother of his friend, lit the cigarette. Lust pulsed through him, hardening his cock. *Fuck, this could get messy.*

Danny swallowed again and a quiver of a smile appeared at the corner of his lips. He wasn't fighting to get his hand back, but he didn't look totally comfortable either.

That's enough for the moment. Go easy.

Marcus pulled away and drew hard on the cigarette. Smoke filled his mouth and he inhaled, his now healthy lungs seizing. He coughed in an uncontrollable spasm, slipping the dart from his mouth in a hurry as he struggled to suck in any clean air.

He glanced up and caught Danny watching him with another one of his devastating, small, sexy smiles.

Marcus laughed but his cheeks grew hot in an embarrassed blush. "What can I say? It's been too long."

He shrugged and took another drag on the cigarette, shallower this time. The nicotine slowly made its way into his starved system, tingling along once-known pleasure centers. He threw his head back and groaned loudly. "Thank you, I so needed that."

Danny returned to the garden bench, dropping down with casual elegance.

"Are you a work friend of Sienna's, Marcus?"

Marcus shook his head and pushed one hand into his front jeans pocket, pushing it down to make the waistband lower and reveal a glimpse of his flat tummy.

Danny's gaze swung down, and he shifted on the seat.

Yep, I'm not wrong about him.

"No, a university friend actually. We only catch up a couple of times a year, which is a shame. She's a good chick." Marcus took another drag of his cigarette and realized he was beginning to enjoy it. *Damn.* It looked like the years of abstinence hadn't quenched his appetite for them after all.

"You here with your girlfriend? How does she feel about Sienna?" Danny's question surprised him, and he couldn't help a grin spreading over his face.

Young and full of confidence, this one. He liked that. Fearless, too, which gave him hope that they'd make it past this one conversation.

"No, no girlfriend. And if I did have a partner, they wouldn't care about Sienna, though she is gorgeous."

Marcus deliberately drew out the moment of truth, curious to see what the youngster would do. Danny's mouth tightened in an uncomfortable way, which made him extremely pleased. He'd hooked Danny's interest, now he just had to wait for him to ask the question that hung in the air.

"Your girlfriends don't get jealous?"

Marcus chuckled and smiled his most charming smile at Danny. The smile that made most guys melt. "I'm gay. I haven't dated a chick in almost ten years. They never really did it for me anyway."

Danny nodded and reached for another cigarette, his hands shaking as he slid another from its case. Well, that wasn't exactly the response Marcus had been hoping for, but at least there was a reaction.

Marcus heard someone approaching and turned toward the newcomer. He couldn't decide if they had good timing or bad. Either way, his exclusive time with Danny had just drawn to a close.

"Hey, Marcus, long time no see!"

Marcus couldn't stop the smile that spread across his face seeing Sienna's long-time best friend Lauren round the hedge. "Hey, Loz! Yeah, I know."

Lauren's glance shifted between Marcus and Danny, eyebrows drawing together in confusion, then her gaze settled on the cigarettes.

"Your mother will kill you if she sees you doing that, Danny!"

Marcus grinned as Danny blushed, his gorgeous eyes sparkling with mutiny.

"Don't you dare say anything."

Marcus had finished his cigarette and pushed the butt into his now empty beer bottle. "Thanks for the smoke, Danny. Lauren, introduce me to this husband of yours." Marcus grabbed Lauren by the hand and dragged her away from Danny for his new friend's sake. There was nothing worse than having a pseudo-big sister looking over your shoulder when you were just coming into your own.

It was hard to leave the only guy he'd wanted in months, though. Actually, it had been probably longer than that. A year, maybe.

Lauren giggled on their walk back into the brightly lit area of the party, pulling him over to a plain, older man with kind eyes.

"Marcus, this is my husband, Jerry."

Marcus smiled and played the part of good friend and token gay guy as he chatted with Lauren's accountant husband. But the conversation didn't stop all his senses from being on high alert for the blond hottie who might have the most beautiful eyes he had ever seen.

Chapter Two

DANNY MOVED around his sister's party as though on autopilot, filling drinks, smiling, and laughing with friends and strangers alike. Being the dutiful son and brother was a role he filled well. Meanwhile, he throbbed with awareness and suppressed lust. He tried to process the reason he'd reacted in that way toward Marcus. Marcus was extremely attractive to him. No one he'd previously encountered had ever come close to affecting him life this. His heart had pounded in his chest like a mallet against stone when Marcus had lit his cigarette only inches from his. He was so bloody hot! But what could he do about it?

Ever since he'd first slept with a girl during his first spring break, he'd wondered what the hell all the fuss was about. Sure, it felt good, but it wasn't exactly earth-shattering. He'd tried again, then again, with different types of girls. Thinner, bigger, sassy, quiet. No one really turned him on, and he just went through the motions, waiting for the anticipated level of excitement to finally kick in.

When he'd gotten hard over the *men* in a porno rather than the women, he'd been terrified of being different. Gay. A queer. Then the fear of the unknown had turned into a craving to discover the truth, to figure out what he needed. His idea of sex was obviously different to all the other guys he knew, but how would he find out if he really was gay? All his friends were straight, and he certainly didn't want to just turn up at an all-male club to find out.

Who would think his sister's thirtieth could be the answer to his prayers?

The speeches moved slowly as they always did at family parties. From where he stood near the bar, he could see Marcus in the opposite corner of the room lounging idly by the food table, staring at him. His stomach turned over every single time Marcus smiled at him. Could a man that much older and so gorgeous really be interested in him?

Danny found it hard to believe, but he sure hoped so. Marcus was a walking wet dream. His thick brown hair fell almost to his shoulders and Danny ached to touch it. He had warm, chocolate brown eyes, and a strong jaw, which, in total, gave him a beautiful face. If the way his clothing clung to him was any indication, Marcus also had a perfectly sculpted body. A shiver of awareness and arousal coursed through him. He had to find a way to be alone with Marcus once more. In fact, he should have done something the first time they'd been together.

Fuck! That's what you get for being a coward.

When the party was finally over and almost everyone had left, it was time to clean up. Marcus had volunteered to stick around to help, which had shocked them all. Butterflies jostled in Danny's stomach at the prospect of being able to talk to him again. But how?

As time ticked by and Danny worked together with his dad to clean the outdoor area, he could no longer ignore the tight band of unease squeezing his chest. The closer they got to finishing, the more the confusion over his sexuality came to the forefront of his mind. Was he or wasn't he?

To be honest, his confusion wasn't the cause of his uneasiness. Yes, he would be terrified of following a completely new and uncertain path. But at this very moment what really worried him was that if Marcus left, he may never see him again.

As he picked up another discarded drink from the ground, his mum interrupted his thoughts. "Danny, could you take all the recycling down to the bins?"

He groaned at the four boxes full of beer and wine bottles next to his mother. "Sure, Mum. I may just need to do four trips, but no problem."

A large, warm body moved up beside him.

"I'll help. Here." Marcus picked up two of the boxes with ease and looked at Danny with a blank expression.

"Which way is it?"

Danny's cheeks burned hot with Marcus staring at him like he didn't even know him. How did he do that?

His cock began to thicken, and he inhaled sharply though his nose. He needed to hide somewhere before his mum saw. Like, now. "Just down the blind side of the house. Out there and turn left."

Marcus nodded and headed out the door without looking back.

Danny took a deep breath and picked up the remaining two boxes in a hurry.

"You all right with those, mate?" His mum had concern written all over her face.

He bit back a sarcastic retort. He was twenty-one, not twelve. "Yeah, Mum, no problem."

He headed out the door, stumbling a little in his eagerness to follow Marcus. The sound of crashing glass filled the space ahead of him as Marcus threw the bottles into the bins.

As he stepped further into the darkness, Danny's stomach tightened like a coiled spring. He tried not to think about how much he wanted Marcus to desire him. He emptied the bottles into the bin and placed the boxes down next to it.

It was dark but he could see that Marcus was only a foot away.

"Thanks for that." He tried for cool, but his voice squeaked.

"No problem." Marcus turned to move back to the house and Danny panicked. Without thinking, he grabbed Marcus' arm.

"Wait—"

Marcus pushed him up against the fence, pressed his hard body against his, and kissed him. Shock made him gasp and tense up against the onslaught. Then he felt Marcus's cock harden against his thigh, hot, and long.

Danny moaned and let his body relax into the kiss. Marcus pressed open his lips and slowly dipped his tongue into his mouth. He slid his arms around Marcus' body and the man grabbed him by the ass, hauling him close.

God, this feels good.

Danny sighed. His cock swelled and lengthened rapidly as their tongues met and thrust against one another. This was the sort of reaction he had always expected and wanted with the girls he'd been with. Was this who and what he needed?

He pulled back from the scorching, hot lips Marcus had on him, panting hard from both lust and confusion. "I don't... I'm not...."

Marcus stepped back instantly, and a pang of regret hit Danny like a fist to the gut. He hadn't meant it as a rejection.

"You don't want me?" Marcus' voice dropped to a whisper. His words were gently spoken and yet Danny could hear the barely controlled steel beneath them.

He swallowed and shrugged, not sure how to answer. His eyes had become accustomed to the dark now and he could see the set of Marcus' strong features. A muscle ticked angrily in his clenched jaw. *Crap.*

"I don't know. I've never..."

Marcus took another step back and turned on his heel, walking back to the house in long, fast strides. Danny could almost feel the vibrations of anger pouring off him.

"It's fine, Danny. Really."

Panic gripped him and he ran after Marcus, his heart hammering in his chest, his breath catching in his throat. This time, he grabbed Marcus' huge shoulder hard and pulled him around. How could he not understand?

"I haven't come out, Marcus!"

Marcus gave him a hard look, squared his shoulders and spread his legs. "Come here."

Danny hesitated for one heartbeat and then stepped closer, lifting his face.

Marcus dragged him into his arms, intense brown eyes looking down upon him as though they could read him.

"Kiss me."

Danny took a quick breath and focused on the man in front of him. He was aware that they were very close to the corner of the house and in view of everyone, but if he looked away, he'd lose this guy for sure. He closed his eyes and brought his lips to meet Marcus' delicious mouth. His belly jumped like a caged animal fighting to get out of his body. Marcus didn't take over, but rather simply held the kiss as it was and Danny became frustrated, wanting the same passion from before.

He moaned, low in his throat, hoping the noise would inspire something. It did.

Marcus wrapped his big arms around his back and Danny moved his hands up, threading his fingers into the thick brown hair he'd been longing to touch.

It was long seconds before Marcus broke off the most heated kiss of Danny's life. He took a step back, hitting the side of the house as the world tipped on its axis.

"I thought you didn't know what to do." Marcus stared at him intently.

Danny smiled and leaned against the bricks for support. He

couldn't help the pride that rose up inside him. "I just followed your lead."

Marcus glanced away and said, "You don't know what you've started, Danny. I want so much more than just a kiss from you."

A lump formed in Danny's throat, but he swallowed it down. "Like what?"

Marcus pointed to the fence next to them, his voice low and menacing.

"Put your hands against the fence and I'll show you."

Fear hit Danny at the same time as a huge wave of lust, and the hairs on his arms prickled into goose bumps. He wouldn't have consciously been able to say which feeling was stronger, but as he moved across the laneway and placed his hands on the fence, he knew his lust had won out.

Marcus stepped up behind him and put his large hands next to Danny's on the wooden palings, his soft skin pressed against Danny's cheek. His breath was hot on his ear and his pelvis pushed against his ass, making his body ache and long for deeper contact.

Danny bit his lip in an attempt to stifle his moans. He was horny beyond bearing, but that was a relief after waiting so long for this sort of intensity.

Marcus thrust his hips, his hard cock pressing between Danny's buttocks. He gasped at the blatant show of intent, but instead of being repulsed, he tilted his pelvis back for Marcus in invitation. He wanted more.

Marcus groaned in his ear. It was the hottest sound he'd ever heard, at least until Marcus whispered to him, "I want you, Danny. I don't care if you've never been with a man before, I'd love to be your first. But I won't touch you unless you want me to. Tell me to stop and I will."

Danny dropped his head back on Marcus's shoulder. Marcus just kept going, thrusting into him and talking dirty, the perfect combination to obliterate any reservations.

"I want to be inside your ass, Danny. Do you understand that? I can't be near you and not want that."

An involuntary shiver slid over Danny and shaking, he closed his eyes. What Marcus was doing to him felt incredible and so *right*.

Marcus kissed Danny's cheek, his lips soft and wet, then he slowly withdrew.

The loss of Marcus' heat and strength devastated him, his stomach dropping in a sickening lurch. Danny bit his lip to stop reacting, embarrassed to be craving it again so quickly. He turned his head to watch Marcus leave him and walk slowly towards the light, adjusting his jeans as he went.

"Fuck, I need another minute." Marcus turned and strode back to him, his chest heaving. "I'm as hard as a rock."

Danny turned around and fell back against the fence, resisting the urge to put his hands behind his back like a naughty child. He wanted to reach forward and stroke Marcus' hard dick and find out just how loud he could be when he came.

The second the thought crossed his mind, Danny's cheeks heated. Where had those feelings come from? He should be more scared of what would happen and worried if people found out. He wasn't, though. The possibility of being with Marcus exited and aroused him so much his nipples tightened beneath his shirt.

He cleared his throat, aiming for a confident tone despite the fact he wasn't feeling anything near it.

"I don't know what to do or say, Marcus. Sorry."

Marcus frowned and rubbed a hand over his face.

"I know. I'm sorry. I'm not helping you like I should be. Look, I'm an avid Essendon supporter. You?"

Danny smiled at the change in topic. Only a man like Marcus could do that incredibly smooth move so easily. From dirty talk to Australian Football League. How did that slide into their conversation? *Only one way to find out.*

"Carlton."

Marcus laughed.

"Perfect. I'm having some friends over on Friday night. Essendon's playing Carlton at the MCG. We'll watch the game, have a few beers, chew the fat. How 'bout you come over and hang around for a bit after? If you want to stay the night, you can. If you don't, no stress."

The gorgeous man shrugged and grinned at him, coinciding with a returning wave of fear, strong and fast. He wanted him to *stay* the night? Who else would be there? "All gay guys?"

Marcus tilted his dark head back toward the house to indicate he wanted to move and began walking back into the light.

Danny followed close behind, glad his throbbing erection had subsided. He couldn't go back to help his parents walking like a cowboy.

They stepped into the backyard and Marcus stood back from the door and dropped his voice to a whisper.

"No, it's a group of work friends. There's six of us. Two of them are gay, including me, the other four are all straight. They're a good bunch of guys."

Danny swallowed the urge to ask if the straight guys minded him being gay, but the thought was pretty apparent. Obviously, they didn't, or they wouldn't be coming over to Marcus' home in the first place.

He had to find out if this was what he needed, who he was. He was petrified, yes, but after literally *years* of questions, what sort of pussy would he be if he didn't take the chance being offered to him?

He drew a deep breath and met Marcus' gaze. "Yeah, that sounds good. Do you want to text me the time and your address, so I have it?"

Marcus' full lips curled into a smile as he pulled out his phone. Thankfully, he didn't comment on the fact that Danny had glossed over the embarrassing exchanging of numbers conversation. He hated that part.

"Sure. Call your phone with mine and then you'll have my number and I'll have yours."

Danny took the offered iPhone and did as the beautiful man in front of him requested. As he tried to inhale, his breath caught. Why had he become so excited?

"Danny, can you come help me with the last of the furniture? Then, I think we're done."

Danny turned toward his mother's voice and tried really hard not to blush.

"Sure, Mum."

He turned back to the brown-eyed god of a man who was still watching him. "Nice to meet you, Marcus."

Marcus nodded and smiled his gentle smile.

"Yeah, you too."

Danny forced himself to head back inside. He heard his mother thank Marcus for all of his help and used every bit of self-preservation he possessed to continue working. He moved the furniture as directed by his dad, then watched as his sister bounced outside to give Marcus a big hug.

Jealousy swept through him like a sickening plague, making his stomach lurch and his hands clench into fists. He ground his teeth in anger, toward both himself and his family for making this so difficult. If Marcus had been a beautiful girl, he wouldn't have worried about chatting with her, flirting, even kissing her if he really liked her. But, no, because Marcus was a man, he had to hide like a rabbit in a hunter's sights.

His parents were going to kill him if they found out. They believed being gay was a lifestyle choice and such people had no rights to anything "normal" people had. No right to be married, no right to have children. They thought being gay meant one was a bad person.

Half of his friends would probably disown him too. They

thought all gay guys wanted to hit on *them*, thus they were the enemy. Ignorant idiots.

He had a lot to think about between now and next Friday night, but he knew one thing. All bets were off when it came to this man, the first male Danny had ever truly wanted. He would keep his mind open to all possibilities and follow his instincts. After all, it was better to ask for forgiveness later than beg for permission now.

Chapter Three

DANNY PUSHED his hands against the steering wheel. He'd sat outside Marcus's place like a dummy in his bloody car for too long.

You're an idiot.

He closed his eyes and forced himself to take a deep, slow breath, letting the tension drain from his overly tight shoulders. "Aw, shit."

Nervous excitement coursed through him as he gripped the steering wheel and looked down at the bulge in his jeans. He hadn't even seen Marcus in person yet, but boy had he been dreaming about him, and it showed. "Come on, you idiot."

Danny huffed, pulled the keys from the ignition, and forced himself out of the car. He jogged up the steps to Marcus's apartment. Step by step, his heart rate accelerated. It had to be the top floor, of course.

He reached the concrete floor on Marcus's level and stopped, glancing around at the silver mirrors and well cared for halls.

Wow, this guy has money.

He liked the fact that Marcus was successful. It meant he was intelligent, driven.

I wonder what he does?

Danny grimaced at the thought. He didn't even know what the man did for a living and yet here he was, on a pseudo first date.

His breathing quickened once again as he pulled out his phone and glanced at the text message for the two hundredth time.

Top floor, apartment seven.

He glanced up at the door he had stopped in front of, the silver number seven enough to make his knees a little weak. Yep, this was it.

It had been a long week of contemplating his feelings and although he was a little scared of what the future may hold, he had ultimately decided that he couldn't keep feeling like half of his soul was missing.

Resolved now thanks to his own little pep talk, he lifted his hand and knocked on the door, hearing someone yell out through the wood almost immediately. The door flew open, revealing a gorgeous blond man, about Marcus's age and height. He wore a pale pink t-shirt and tight jeans. Marcus had said there was another gay man at the party. It looked like he'd had found him. Or more accurately, the man had found Danny.

"Hey, you must be Danny."

He nodded and smiled. "Yep, that's me.

The blond hunk returned the smile and indicated he should come in.

"I'm Thomas, by the way."

Danny turned and extended his hand. "Nice to meet you."

Thomas gripped his hand, shook it weakly, and eyed him appreciatively.

"You're really cute. Where did Marcus find you?"

Stumped for an answer, all that came out of his mouth was, "Ummm."

Luckily, Marcus strolled in at that exact moment, saving him from the huge task of dealing with his first chat with an effeminate man.

"He's Sienna's brother, Tommy. Stop interrogating him. Hey,

Danny." Marcus turned his beautiful brown eyes on him, and Danny's knees went shaky.

"Beer?" Marcus held up a cold, freshly opened bottle.

Danny didn't really like beer, but he grabbed it for something to do with his hands. "Yeah, sure. Thanks."

Marcus's hot, muscular arm wrapped around his shoulders and steered him toward the lounge room, which was a huge, open plan area. His warmth and touch were lovely, and Danny missed them the moment Marcus's arm dropped away.

Four other guys were lying over the sofas, watching the pre-game show.

Wow, beautiful furniture, huge space. Perfect for entertaining.

"Hey, guys, this is Danny. Danny, the guys."

Danny waved. "Hi."

Marcus patted him on the ass and the playful gesture made him jump. His light tap sent goose bumps racing along his skin and blood pumping to his groin. Was that sort of touching allowed in front of everyone?

"Go grab a seat. The game's about to begin."

Danny found a solitary chair and Marcus climbed onto one of the empty sofas. He wanted to go over and sit with him, but should he? This wasn't a date. His legs took on a will of their own and shifted restlessly beneath him. He swiveled the bottle between his hands and the coldness seeped in to numb his skin.

Should I go? Or would that be too obvious?

Just as he got the courage to lift up off the chair, Thomas came back into the room and jumped into the empty seat next to Marcus.

Marcus glanced up and met Danny's eyes, his eyebrows raised in silent question.

Not sure how to answer, his immediate response was to shake his head and concentrate on the football. It was Essendon versus Carlton, a brilliant match. The first half passed quickly, and Carlton was up by one goal. He was rapt and cheering loudly, but the rest of the guys were groaning.

"You ordered the pizzas, Marcus?" one of the men asked.

Marcus' brown eyes shifted down to his phone. "Yeah, sent the order off half an hour ago. They should be here soon."

As though his words had caused the delivery to magically appear, the doorbell rang. Marcus went to get up but two of the other guys jumped to their feet.

"Nah, it's our turn to shout. You've got the last couple."

Marcus opened his mouth to obviously disagree, his brow furrowing over his eyes, but they were gone.

Danny's gaze dragged back to Marcus and smiled. He loved generosity in a person. It was just another ticked box.

"So, how old are you Danny?" Thomas asked, a weird grin on his rather cute face.

Danny grimaced, the hairs on the back of his neck prickling. He didn't like Thomas's voice. It was a little too high, and the pitch was annoying. As were his questions.

"Twenty-one," Danny answered honestly with a grin. He was in his prime sexually, or so they said.

Marcus gave a grunt of disapproval and slapped Thomas's thigh. "That was rude."

"How is that rude?" Thomas scoffed. "I bet you didn't even know that."

Marcus's gaze shifted back to Danny, his heated brown eyes causing Danny's cheeks to heat. They knew so little about each other but the attraction that burned between them was intense.

"You working or studying, Danny?" Thomas drifted his hand over Marcus's hair and stroked it with casual ease.

Marcus frowned and swatted him away, which was good to see, but Danny found it distracting. Couldn't they stop playing like that in front of him?

"I'm at University for another year."

Thomas moved gracefully and draped his legs over Marcus's lap. Marcus looked up again with an uncomfortable pull around his mouth, but he didn't move them away.

Anger surged through him and his belly dropped dangerously, and he pulled clenched fists into his lap to hide them.

"What are you studying at University, Danny?"

"Structural engineering," he spat out.

Would Thomas stop touching Marcus like that? His pulse raced and he panted as if running a race, and yet he had done nothing but sit and stare at them.

Thomas poked Marcus in the shoulder with his finger, his mouth transforming into a grin.

"How perfect."

Danny stared at the two men, his chest tightening the moment the truth settled in. They obviously knew each other well.

Unable to stay ambivalent to the source of their humor, he forced his mouth into a smile. "Why's that?"

Marcus smiled at him with his lips but it didn't really light up his eyes, and he shifted as though uncomfortable on the sofa.

"Because, I'm an architect. You could probably come and do an internship with me next year."

Danny shook his head. There was no chance of that. Even if something did out of this mess, he wouldn't like working under someone he had known intimately.

The men returned with the pizza and lay out the hot, fragrant food. The smell of cheese and toppings filled the air. They all ate and talked about the football scores, then who the teams should trade, which coaches they liked. It would have been any other normal guys' night of football, except for the deep sense of disappointment settling into Danny's gut, and making the pizza sit badly in his stomach. He hadn't been honest with himself before. He had thought he'd be fine with just waiting and seeing what happened, but he wasn't.

He needed Marcus to want *him,* not Thomas. Jealousy was ripping his insides apart.

The second half passed much slower. Essendon lost their momentum and fell behind. Thomas, the ignorant little shit, cheered even harder. When he wasn't caressing Marcus, that was.

He noticed Marcus didn't return any of the touches, but it was obvious he was used to such attention. Were they a couple? Casual fuck buddies? He had to bite the inside of his mouth to stop himself from screaming the questions out loud.

What are they?

Either way, friends or lovers, he didn't plan on staying around to find out.

When the football finished, the men soon picked up their phones, keys, and wallets, then headed for the door.

"Nice to meet you," Danny responded calmly to most of their goodbyes, but his arms shook from the adrenaline pumping through him. He needed to leave and couldn't believe he had actually thought Marcus wanted him.

"You aren't staying?" Marcus moved toward the front door.

He turned to face his tormentor. Why had Marcus invited him over if only to tease him? His chest ached just from the stress of breathing. His stomach had clenched tight.

"No, I think Thomas wants to stay. Three's a crowd." Danny couldn't stop the venomous words escaping from his mouth. He didn't want to sound like an angry child, but fuck, was he mad.

"Oh, jealous, are you? Are you always going to be like that?" Marcus cocked his head and his brown eyes moved over his face in an assessing way.

"I'm not bloody jealous. It's just obvious that you two are fucking, so I might as well leave." Danny tried to move past him, but the big idiot stood his ground.

Marcus smiled a really irritatingly pleased smile.

"Oh, I like this side of you, Danny."

Furious now, he growled and clenched his teeth so hard his jaw ached. He needed to get out of there. He went to move forward but Marcus backed him up against a wall and gripped both his hands, lifting them up near his head.

He fought to pull his arms down, but he literally couldn't as Marcus's body was pinning him in place. He glared up at the man who held him effortlessly against the wall. "Let me go, Marcus."

"Where are you going, Danny?" Marcus' brown eyes held concern, but there was something else there, too.

"Home. I don't want to stay."

Marcus' gaze narrowed and he pressed his pelvis closer, as if making sure Danny felt him, and he did. Too much. His cock ached to be touched and he swallowed hard as he attempted to keep up the level of anger in his glare.

"But I want you to stay."

Danny groaned and turned his head away. Marcus twisted his pelvis from side to side, using his hard cock to rub against Danny's groin and he hardened instantly.

"No!" He groaned against the conflicting emotions and tugged at the hands that held him. Marcus was too strong, and he couldn't free himself. He should have been a little scared, but he wasn't.

Marcus bent his head forward and licked a wet path down the skin just below his ear. Danny shivered and bit his lip as a wave of heat and longing flooded over him. What was it about this guy that made him want Marcus so badly?

"I want you Danny, so much. I want to suck your cock. I want to fuck your ass. I want to listen to you scream as you come over and over again. Are you sure you don't want that too?"

Danny's eyes slid shut and his arousal hitched up another notch. His breathing came in a labored, panting rhythm now and his heart beat in heavy, thudding beats. He had never felt like this before.

"Ah... Marcus? I'll see you at work on Monday?"

Danny's eyes flew open and eyed the door. Thomas stood there, looking as embarrassed as he felt. His face grew hot and he averted his gaze.

Danny tried to pull his hands down from their imprisoned position, but Marcus held him tight, not moving an inch.

"Yeah, great. Lock the door and pull it shut, would you, Tommy?" Marcus casually asked his mate while still pinning Danny to the wall.

Triumph hovered on the edge of his consciousness, registering the disappointed look on Thomas' face, but there was just too much going on in his body to appreciate it. Thomas nodded and as he left, they both waited for the door to lock.

Marcus pushed hard into him again.

"I want you now. If you don't, tell me. I can't wait anymore."

Danny turned and glared at him. "What? After ignoring me all night you just want me to jump into bed with you? No way."

Marcus kissed him on the lips hard and fast. He pulled back and returned his glare.

"You're the one who chose the chair, Danny. We'll talk about Tommy later. Tonight is about us. Do you want me or not?"

Danny examined the carpet, heat creeping up his neck and cheeks. He wanted Marcus, but what the hell was he going to do? Biting his lip, he stared into Marcus' brown eyes. "I do, Marcus. But you know I haven't done this before."

Marcus nodded, dropped his dark head and kissed him with hot, deep kisses. His tongue stroked, demanded, conquered, and made him ache for more.

Danny met the kisses with his own passion, and pushed his tongue into Marcus' mouth, moaning into the heat between them.

When Marcus released his wrists, Danny groaned in relief. His arms dropped down and he ran his hands down Marcus's body.

He grabbed at the hem of Marcus's t-shirt and hauled it up, breaking their kiss to pull the cotton up and off his lover's body.

Wow.

Marcus', upper torso was incredible, and his mouth watered as he stared at the flesh he'd unveiled. Large pecs, small pink nipples, massive arms, and a stomach so hard and flat he wanted to kiss every inch. Marcus had a light sprinkling of brown chest hair, which made him look even more mature and manly. How much time did he put in at the gym to look like this?

Marcus reached for Danny's t-shirt and paused as if waiting for permission, his brown eyes vulnerable and needy. They took his breath away.

Danny gathered his nerve and nodded, lifting his arms once more. He would need a lot of courage before the end of the night.

Marcus stripped off his t-shirt and grinned, running his hands over Danny's chest. His sensitive nipples pulsed when Marcus squeezed them.

Then Marcus dropped to his knees.

"What...?" Danny started to ask. But he fell silent, watching Marcus undo the button of his jeans, work the fly down over his erection, then slip the jeans down his legs.

When Marcus gripped his jocks and pulled them down, he swallowed his apprehension. His cock bounced out, hard and ready. What would Marcus think of his dick? Danny didn't want to be worried about it. He couldn't change it, but still...

"Yum." Marcus grinned up at him and winked.

Heat burned his cheeks and he waited, pleased by Marcus's words. He ached to feel Marcus's mouth around him. But would he do it?

Marcus wrapped his warm hand around the base of Danny's cock and sucked the head into his mouth. Lightning streaks of pleasure pulsed into his balls.

"Oh, fuck!" Danny fell back against the wall and threaded his fingers into Marcus' hair. Sensations unlike any he had ever experienced pierced his brain and flowed out through his body, making every nerve ending hyper-sensitive. His touch was all hot, intense and amazing. Marcus moved faster and harder, using his hand to stroke while his lips sucked and toyed with the head.

He was going to come too soon.

"Marcus." Danny tugged hard on Marcus's hair, but his lover moaned and moved faster.

"Stop, please." Danny began to pant. His balls tightened. "I'm going to come."

Marcus hummed and sucked harder. Oh, wow, did that mean that he wanted to swallow him?

Fuck that's hot.

Danny grabbed a tighter hold on Marcus' head and let his orgasm come. His balls tightened, sensation pierced his belly and heat shot up his shaft. His seed pulsed up and out of him as heat spread down his legs.

He moaned, loudly.

"Fuck. Oh, *fuck*. That is so good."

Marcus continued to milk him with his hot hands and mouth until he could barely stand, his legs like jelly.

Marcus finally stood up, his face alight, happy.

"That was awesome. You taste brilliant." He leaned forward and kissed him on the lips, his energy apparent in his quick movements.

Marcus' hard-on was still pushing through his jeans and despite the lethargy pulling at his body, he reached down to stroke him over the denim.

"What about you?"

Marcus grinned like the devil himself, his eyes alight with mischief. "Come to bed with me?"

Chapter Four

MARCUS REGARDED Danny's wide eyes as he absorbed his words, then he swallowed hard. Would he do it?

He'd never had a gay virgin and it aroused him something fierce. Danny had obviously been with girls, but there was a reason he'd come here now. He needed something different, and his cock ached to give it to him.

Danny nodded slowly, his blue eyes wary.

Poor kid doesn't even know what he's agreeing to.

Marcus groaned, his patience hanging by a thread, and grabbed Danny's hand. "Get rid of the shoes."

Danny glanced down and shimmied out of his jeans and runners. Marcus grunted and pulled him by the hand, naked, along the hall to his room. He would need to be gentle and would have to talk to him and explain things. Two things he found difficult to do in bed.

They stepped into Marcus' bedroom and he twisted around, opened his jeans and pushed them down his legs, then stood back up. He hadn't bothered with underwear.

Danny's eyes bulged at his cock. Being larger than most men didn't really mean anything, but now Danny was looking scared.

"You're huge."

Marcus held out a hand to his young lover. "Come touch me. We'll take this slow." Even if it was going to kill him, he would do it. For Danny.

His cock stood up, completely hard, the tip red and throbbing with need, his balls painfully tight. He wouldn't last long.

Danny wrapped his hand tentatively around him. Marcus moaned with each hesitant stroke. He threw his head back and thrust his cock forward. "That feels so good."

He lowered his head again and saw Danny's face. His eyes were wide, but his lips were smiling. He was enjoying himself.

"Lie on your back, Danny."

Danny gazed over at the bed and released Marcus' cock from his tight fist. He crawled onto the mattress, his tight, gorgeous ass flashing in all its glory for only a moment before he lay on one of the pillows.

"Like this?"

Marcus smiled and pure pleasure spread through him like warm sunshine. He was enjoying Danny's innocence a little too much. "Yes."

Marcus joined him on the bed, crawling up and laying on top of his young lover in an attempt to be as close to him as possible. Their bodies met and heat spread through him.

"God, you feel good," he said through clenched teeth and struggled to hold onto some control. He wanted to lift up Danny's leg, thrust in, and give in to the need of his body to fuck him hard and fast until they both came. But he had to take his time and ease him into it.

Go slow!

He bent his head and kissed Danny, their tongues entwining in a most intimate kiss. He broke off, panting, his cock weeping precum as he rocked against Danny's hot, young body.

"I'm never going to last if we keep this up."

There was something so strange about those kisses. They aroused him to the point of breaking, the intimacy of such a simple thing amazing.

A small smile spread across Danny's lips.

"That's probably a good thing."

Danny's fear went through him like it was his own and he caressed the younger man's body in an attempt to calm him.

"You are gorgeous, Danny. I've wanted to do this since the first minute I saw you." He moved lower and sucked Danny's nipple into his mouth.

Danny groaned and grabbed at his arms.

Marcus alternated a trail of kisses and bites all the way down Danny's chest, trying to give him as much pleasure as possible. Danny's cock was lengthening again, and Marcus smiled to himself. It was one of the great things about a young lover... he'd never recover half as fast as Danny.

"I see you need some more attention," Marcus addressed Danny's cock, before he took it once again in his mouth—something he didn't generally do often.

Marcus was a top, the dominant partner. He preferred to be catered to and almost always received the sucking and did the fucking. But for some reason, giving Danny pleasure was a need he couldn't deny.

He hummed and went to work on Danny's hardening flesh, smiling as it grew, lengthening and thickening beneath his ministrations.

"Marcus," Danny groaned his name and tugged on his hair.

Already? Good boy.

Marcus released Danny's now hard cock and came back up to his lover's flushed face. He kissed Danny again, biting his juicy bottom lip, trying desperately to ignore the throbbing between his legs.

When Danny lifted his knees and wiggled a bit, he nearly shot his load.

"Do you want me to do anything?"

Marcus shook his head and groaned. "No. Just as long as you're sure?"

Danny nodded and trailed his damp fingers down Marcus' chest, pinching his nipples as he went.

"I'm sure."

Marcus cursed in frustration and rolled off the bed. The one thing about needing protection was that it really wrecked the mood.

"Where are you going?" Danny sat up, disappointment obvious in his gorgeous pout.

Marcus reached into a drawer for lube and a condom. "We need these. Don't *ever* let anyone fuck you without both."

Danny flushed red and his eyes looked hurt.

"I don't want anyone else to fuck me," he huffed then lay back down, crossing his arms over his chest.

Marcus mentally slapped himself. Not something to mention to a first timer.

He slid a condom over his weeping cock and spread lube over the tip.

Then he crawled back onto the bed, kneeled between Danny's legs, and glanced down into his blue eyes. His lover needed to feel special and he wanted to give that to him. "Danny, I don't ever go down on anyone and I've sucked your cock twice. I've never swallowed, yet I did for you. Believe me, you're something very special. I don't want anyone fucking you except me, either."

Oh, wow.

He hadn't meant to say that much.

Danny's blue eyes looked vulnerable as his hands slid up Marcus' arms.

"And I only want you. Be careful, though."

Marcus lifted Danny's knees up closer to his chest and applied lube to his ass.

"It always hurts a little. That's part of it. But I promise you'll grow to love it."

He tapped his fingertip against Danny's star and slid a finger into his ass. Danny arched his back and moaned. When Marcus added a second finger and deliberately massaged his prostate, Danny's eyes widened, and his mouth dropped open.

"That feels so weird."

Marcus moved his fingers in and out, scissoring, stretching the virgin tissues. His cock bobbed in anticipation of being inside such a tight ass. He clenched his teeth, his patience slipping.

"But good, yeah?" he forced out, adding more lube to his fingers.

Danny locked eyes with him and nodded.

"Yes. Do you want me to flip over?"

Marcus shook his head. Usually that was easiest, but not tonight. It would be far too impersonal, too. "No, I want to watch your face."

He removed his fingers, lined up his cock, and slid the head in. Tight heat engulfed him, and he bit back a groan as his cock pulsed with the sensation.

"Fuck. That hurts." Danny squeezed his eyes shut and grabbed a hold of the covers either side of him. His legs were shaking and his whole body was tight.

"Just breathe, Danny," Marcus soothed and rocked his hips, slowly moving forward until he slid completely inside his lover.

Danny gasped and wiggled against him. The motions only increased Marcus's arousal, and sweat formed on his forehead and back from the strain of not moving.

He took a deep breath and fell forward inches away from Danny's strained face, then froze in place. He was so good, so damn tight, but he couldn't continue without making sure his lover was all right.

"Babe, look at me."

Danny opened his eyes, pain evident in their blue depths.

"Just relax. Stroke your cock and kiss me. You feel amazing."

Marcus pulled out almost to the tip and slid back in slowly. Danny gasped and reached up to pull Marcus down to him. He kissed him hungrily while thrusting slowly, loving the heat and tightness engulfing him.

He pushed up with his arms, separating their bodies for a moment and moving slowly in and out. *Wow.*

"Tug on your cock, Danny."

Danny flushed, his eyes glazing over.

"It's starting to feel really good."

Marcus groaned and began to pump faster, moving his hips harder and groaning as the tightness around his cock squeezed him. "I know, but I want you to come again too."

Danny reached down and began moving his hand against his length, brushing his knuckles against Marcus' abs as he did.

Marcus gazed down and his gut tightened. "I love seeing you do that. I'm going to ask you to pull your cock just for me later."

He thrust harder and faster, snapping his hips and relishing the sounds of slapping skin in the otherwise quiet room. His orgasm roared down on him, every muscle in his belly tightening in need. He didn't want his lover to miss out.

"Come, Danny, please... I need to watch your face this time."

He pushed Danny's legs up higher, changed his angle, and a heartfelt roar from Danny rewarded him.

"Yes. Oh fuck, *yes!* There."

Danny began to tremble. *Fuck! Please. I can't hold on much longer.*

"I'm coming!"

Danny's blue eyes glazed over and his face flushed with blood. Hot cum burst over their bodies and Marcus moaned, the reins on his control finally slipping from his grasp.

"Yes," he growled out as he fucked Danny with hard pistoning of his hips. His balls tightened and his seed boiled, exploding into

Danny's hot, convulsing channel. The spasms went on and on, tingling along his arms, his legs.

Fucking hell. That truly was mind-blowing sex.

He kissed Danny once more, pulled out gently, and moved off the bed. Danny gasped and stretched, his face contorting in odd spasms for a moment before relaxing once again. Marcus had to leave him for a minute to clean up, and strode straight into his en suite, washed himself then wet a face towel with warm water.

He shook his head as he stared into the mirror for a moment, unable to believe what had just transpired. That was one of the best sessions of his life. His orgasm had been shattering—his hands still shook. Yet, he expected that with Danny, these sensations were only the beginning.

He stumbled back into his bedroom to find Danny still lying on his back panting, both hands on his fast rising and falling belly. He climbed onto the bed and wiped down Danny's abs and chest.

"Thanks."

Danny's smile was all the thanks he needed, but the words were great for his ego. Marcus threw the face washer in the direction of the bathroom and grinned back. His legs ached, as did the rest of his body, so he let himself roll, collapsing onto his back and pulling Danny's warm body into his arms.

Danny settled his head onto Marcus' chest, settling in like a cat against him and gently stroking his nipple with a fingertip.

"Was that okay?"

Marcus laughed.

Are you kidding? That was the best orgasm of my life.

When Danny stiffened within his arms Marcus realized he hadn't actually answered.

"Danny, relax. That was incredible. I only laughed because it was way better than 'okay.' Fucking awesome, is more like it."

Danny didn't say anything but pulled up the blanket, reached across Marcus' body and hugged him tight.

Marcus wrapped both arms around his lover and searched inside himself to see how he truly felt. Real intimacy was difficult, and he often felt uncomfortable after sex. Getting up and leaving was a common occurrence.

Sharing one of the most intimate things you could do, often with a complete stranger, left him feeling empty and cold.

But as he held Danny's hot body in his arms and felt his lover's breath on his chest, there was nowhere he would rather be and no one he would prefer to be with.

Marcus lifted a hand to Danny's blond hair and stroked it, enjoying the rest and shared warmth.

"So, you aren't fucking Tommy?"

Danny's voice was barely a whisper, but Marcus heard him and felt his belly clench. He tightened his embrace, knowing that being honest was the only way to handle this, even though Danny may struggle to hear it.

"We had two nights together when we first met, more than five years ago. We're good mates now, which is great because we're much better as friends. Being with him wasn't right. It was horrible, actually."

Danny turned his head and kissed Marcus's sternum, sighing against him. "Thank you."

Marcus grinned, a weight lifting from his chest in the rush of pure relief that had him feeling a little light-headed.

He hadn't felt this happy in... well... probably ever.

Danny's breathing changed and he began to snore lightly. Marcus glanced down and wanted to laugh. He'd passed out already? Well, to be fair, two orgasms in an hour would probably knock just about anyone out.

Marcus could never fall asleep quickly or for very long. He probably should get up and do some work because he had a pretty major deadline due on Tuesday.

In a minute, he promised himself and closed his eyes. Peace and contentment stole over him, washing him into oblivion.

45

Chapter Five

DANNY AWOKE UNUSUALLY warm and in fetal position, sunlight streaming over his face. He blinked at the intrusion and tried to roll onto his back, but he couldn't.

Marcus' hot, large, muscular body was pressed up against him, his arm draped over Danny's waist, holding him possessively.

Last night hit him in a rush, a kaleidoscope of memories flashing though his mind. Marcus' loving attention, his passion. His own pleasure and double orgasm. He had never known anything could feel so good. Being with Marcus was amazing and he had to admit he had loved being fucked by this man last night.

He blushed just thinking it, but it was true. He really had enjoyed having his ass fucked. Heat infused his cheeks and he shook his head against the pillow. How was he ever going to tell his mates about this?

"Oh, wow, is that the time? Good morning," Marcus groaned behind him, thrusting his morning hard-on into his back.

Danny pushed back against his lover, desire lengthening his cock at the offer. He was happy for a repeat performance, and more than once if possible. He could barely feel a twinge from last night's activities and assumed he should have been quite sore.

"Oh, wow, what?"

"I can't believe I slept all night. I never do that." Marcus dropped a light kiss onto Danny's shoulder and snuggled closer.

Danny stiffened, his stomach dropping. Marcus wasn't talking about his past lovers, was he?

"Never sleep with the guys you fuck, you mean?" Danny aimed for a light, even tone, but knew he had failed when Marcus' arm tightened.

"I don't fuck guys in this bed, Danny," he whispered into his ear. "And I meant, I've never sleep so well. I'm usually up half the night working. Then I wake before sunrise."

Marcus moved his hand down to Danny's half stiff cock and squeezed it firmly.

"You must have knocked me out good and proper last night."

Danny turned his head, arched his neck and kissed Marcus's full lips. He moaned as his cock hardened and swelled under Marcus' skillful touch.

He broke their kiss, desire tightening his belly. "It's still early. Let's fuck and pass out again."

Marcus kissed him and rolled away to collect the lube and condoms again, thoughtful man that he was.

"On your knees, Danny. This is going to be a quick, hard ride."

Danny's legs quivered. He rolled onto his stomach and pushed up onto his hands and knees. That didn't sound entirely pleasant.

The mattress sunk as Marcus moved across it again and reached out for him. His warm hands ran down his back and cupped his ass, spreading lube over his hole. The feeling made him yelp a little, but he forced himself to breathe evenly.

"You have the hottest ass, lover."

Danny huffed out a laugh at that. He didn't think so, but he opened his legs wider and tried to relax. It hurt so much less when he wasn't fighting it.

Marcus pressed his cock to Danny's ass and pulled him back onto him. Pain spread through him as if his body wanted to reject Marcus, squeezing tight.

Just focus on something else.

Marcus' hands stroked over his abdomen and he gently rocked his hips. As he pushed further in, Danny's body accepted him, relaxed, and the pain turned into tingles of pleasure.

"Oh, fuck," he moaned out as Marcus lay over his back, the contact hot and electric. It was like being consumed by his lover, protected and encapsulated by him. Marcus reached around and began tugging on his cock. Sensations of pleasure tightened his balls and flooded his belly. Danny pushed up with his arms, holding them both in position. It felt so fucking good.

Marcus began to piston his hips, deep and fast, sweat forming between their connected bodies.

"Are you okay?" he panted, fucking Danny harder.

Danny groaned and dropped his head closer to the mattress. Every time Marcus thrust forward, he pressed on something inside him that caused pleasure to zing around his balls and along his cock. "I'm going to come. Don't stop, Marcus."

As Marcus moved harder and faster, Danny's orgasm roared through him. Marcus pulled his cock again and he screamed. His cum shot out of him in bursts. He fell forward, but Marcus pushed up with his arms and kept riding him hard and fast until he groaned and shuddered.

Danny turned his head and reached around to pull Marcus down further.

"Stay just there for a minute."

Marcus tensed but then slowly relaxed, sinking onto him and pressing kisses to his back. He was heavy but warm, the pressure wonderful.

"I don't want to hurt you."

Danny smiled groggily against the mattress, his brain in bliss. "Mmm, I like it." Relaxed, he almost fell asleep again, the pressure of Marcus' huge body soothing to him.

Marcus stayed like that for long moments, then finally slipped his softened cock free of Danny's body and climbed off the bed. Danny winced and rolled over, the ache in his ass turning into a real throbbing sensation. He would definitely be feeling that later on.

Marcus returned and crawled onto the bed, his smile and red face still intact. Danny forced his sated body onto its side so that Marcus could spoon him again. His lover didn't disappoint him, nestling against his back, his arm sneaking around Danny's middle.

"Thank you," Danny whispered.

Just as sleep enveloped him, he thought he heard Marcus whisper,

"No, thank you."

When Danny next awoke it was to the sound of the shower running. He stretched his arms and groaned. What a wild night. He waited for the guilt, the shame, the feeling of utter wrongness to envelop him. He had just spent a night letting a gorgeous *man* fuck him. How did he feel about that?

Simply put, he had never known anything could feel so good. Though his ass ached like a bitch now.

Danny hauled himself out of bed and staggered down the hall to use the toilet in the other bathroom. Marcus was still in the shower when he returned. It wouldn't hurt to join him, surely?

Danny padded into the bathroom as quietly as possible and smiled at the vision of beauty in the shower. Marcus' silhouette was perfection. Huge shoulders, defined biceps and chest, flat abs and his lovely, cut cock hanging between his legs.

How could a man like that want me?

"Hey, gorgeous. Want to join me?"

Danny smiled and nodded at his lover. "Absolutely!"

He stepped around the solid piece of glass and moved beneath the hot spray.

"What are your plans for the weekend?" Marcus asked while he shampooed his thick, brown hair.

Danny picked up the soap and washed off the sweat, cum and lube. He'd never been so dirty, even when he'd first discovered masturbation.

"A twenty-first tonight, but not much tomorrow."

Marcus moved forward and they changed positions, his lover tilting his head back under the stream of water to wash the suds off. He was beautiful to watch. Strong and confident. Sexy. Very sexy.

But he had a sore ass. He couldn't go another round, even if his horny brain wanted him to. "You?"

Marcus stepped out of the shower and towel dried his muscled body.

"Going to a concert tonight, bit of work tomorrow. Do you want to go out for dinner tomorrow night?"

Danny stared at his new lover, surprise and fear filtering through his system. His chest tightened, his throat constricted. He now knew he was gay. He had to be after what they did last night—and he'd loved every fucking moment. But he wasn't exactly ready to be "out."

"I don't know."

Marcus wrapped a towel around his waist and shook his wet hair. *Damn, the man is hot.*

"Look, Danny, you can just come over here and fuck if that's all you want, but I know you need more than that, and so do I. I won't kiss you in public. Let's just go somewhere casual, have a pizza and chat, then see where we're at."

Hope spread through Danny like wildfire. He hadn't been looking for anything serious when he had come over last night, but now that it was being hinted at, he couldn't wipe the smile off his face. "Yeah, that would be cool."

Marcus laughed and walked out of the bathroom.

Danny stayed under the water and let the heat run over him. His life was changing, and he had no control of it. He'd got on the roller coaster and after the ride of his life, he didn't want to get off.

Sunday night arrived and Danny made an excuse to his parents about having dinner at a mate's house then headed over to Marcus's. His breath kept catching in his throat and his belly leaped like a bloody frog in a pond. If he and Marcus got along well, would he want to keep seeing him? Marcus had said he was happy with the sex and Danny certainly was, but would that be enough to build a relationship on? Did he even want that with the very first guy he'd been with?

Hell, yes!

He climbed the stairs to the top floor, his heart rate rocketing. Dating Marcus was certainly going to help his cardio. He grinned, stepped in front of door number seven, and knocked on the door.

"Pull it together," he whispered to himself as he shoved his hands into his pockets. His hands were literally shaking with excitement.

The door swung open and there was Marcus, shock written all over his face.

"Danny! What's the time?" Marcus asked, realization dawning on his face as his mouth opened wide.

"About six thirty." Danny felt the smile fall from his face. Had Marcus forgotten? *Seriously?*

"Come in, come in." Marcus waved at him, so Danny stepped into the hallway. Should he go?

"I am so sorry, Danny. I've been working all day and I haven't finished. I thought it was still about two."

In the living area there was paper piled high on every surface. He had a better look at Marcus. He wore trackies and an old t-shirt and looked like he hadn't even had a shower.

"I could help if you wanted me to?" The offer was out of his mouth before he could stop it.

Marcus smiled at him.

"I would love that. Though I don't know what you can do."

Danny pulled out his phone. "Well, first of all, when did you last eat?"

Marcus smirked.

"I had a coffee for breakfast."

Danny frowned at his lover. How was he meant to work properly without food? "Do you want Thai or pizza delivered?"

Marcus laughed.

"Thai, please."

Danny called a nearby Thai restaurant and organized for delivery. He wasn't going hungry and neither was Marcus.

"There. Now we can eat something, chat, and you can get your work done."

Marcus was regarding him strangely, his eyes wide and his mouth pulled down a little.

"What's wrong?"

Marcus shook his head and gazed at him as if considering.

"Nothing. I'm just surprised you fixed that so easily."

Danny took his jacket off and shrugged. He'd always been relatively organized and levelheaded. "You need to eat, and we had a date planned anyway. Someone has to make sure you eat something."

Again, Marcus' face looked thoughtful.

"Marcus, what is that expression for?" Danny rolled his eyes at his lover and suppressed the need to shake him. Why wasn't he talking?

Marcus laughed out loud and strode toward him. He kissed Danny on the lips, hard and fast, then pulled back.

"I don't have anyone in my life who looks after me, Danny. It's kind of nice."

Danny stepped away and sat on a stool, glancing toward the ground. "Well, I'm hungry. And you look like shit."

Marcus chuckled and pulled out some drawings, getting Danny's attention and placing them in front of him on the bench.

"Have a look at this. A structural engineer's opinion may be just what I need."

Chapter Six

"MY HEAD IS THROBBING." Marcus put his palm on his pounding forehead.

I need a huge dose of any sort of painkillers.

He wasn't fussy as long as it stopped feeling like someone was hitting his brain with a mallet.

Danny sat up straighter on the couch and put his feet on the floor.

"Come lie down here." Danny patted his lap and Marcus's heart gave a lurch. What was it about this guy that made him want to keep him forever? Maybe it was the selflessness, the giving. So few guys had those traits.

Marcus moved over to the couch, collapsed onto the cushion and groaned. He lay his head down on Danny's lap. "Thank you so much for your help. I would never have finished that project by the deadline if it weren't for you."

"You can pay me back later." Danny chuckled.

He sighed and smiled at the suggested payment. He would love to give Danny anything he liked later.

His headache had instantly lessened in intensity when he lay down, and the relief of getting one mammoth project completed was enough to make him close to passing out. He swung his legs up and curled into fetal position. His eyes fluttered shut the moment Danny stroked his hair.

"That feels so good," he moaned as Danny massaged his scalp. "A guy could get used to this."

Danny laughed softly but didn't say anything. Marcus settled into his lover and the couch more comfortably then lay his hand on Danny's knee. He had wanted to wine and dine his new lover. Leading, of course, to another long night of fucking. That hadn't exactly gone to plan.

"I'm sorry we didn't get to go out for dinner. Not exactly the date I had in mind."

Danny ran one warm hand down Marcus' back and continued stroking his hair. It felt so good, so soothing.

"I don't need to go out. I've had a great time."

Marcus hmphed, not sure he believed that. "Yeah, but I wanted to show you off."

Both of Danny's hands stopped moving instantly, the effect shocking in the way his skin prickled. Marcus pushed back up to sitting, his eyes opening as though they had lead weights attached.

Tension was radiating off Danny and his focus snapped into place immediately, his brain clearing as Danny stared at him.

"You don't like that idea?"

Danny swallowed, regret in his blue eyes.

"I don't know how I'm going to do this. I've never told anyone that I thought I might be... gay. But with you..."

Marcus forced himself to his feet and held out a hand, his brain swimming in low-level pain and exhaustion. He needed sleep.

What they were talking about was an extremely important discussion, but it was too late to decide now. "I'm pretty useless now, but come to bed with me. I missed you last night."

Danny took his hand and they were soon naked, spooning in bed together. A frisson of fear danced around Marcus' brain as he played over their conversation. Holding Danny like this made everything fall into place like a puzzle piece that had been missing all his life. He felt settled, happy. What had happened to him?

He took a deep breath, inhaling the almost sweet smell of Danny's soft skin. A berry fragrance from his hair mingled with the scent of his skin. Intoxicating.

He didn't want to let Danny go but he hadn't been in this position before. Perhaps he just needed to reassure Danny that there was no pressure? After all, they had only known each other a week.

"We don't need to rush this, Danny. You don't have to tell anyone yet. Let's just spend some time together and see how it goes."

Danny grabbed the hand he'd placed around his chest and snuggled closer.

He responded, his cock twitching with need, but his head was still pounding, the pain like knives behind his eyes. He kissed the back of Danny's neck.

"How do you feel about morning sex?"

Danny chuckled.

"With you? Any time works for me."

Marcus grinned before he fell deeply into the land of dreams.

Chapter Seven

MORNING ARRIVED AND MARCUS' head had cleared. *Thank God for that. Nothing worse than a thumping headache to render you almost incapacitated.*

His guest had been wonderful. More than that, Danny had saved his ass. He would probably still be working on that project without Danny's help and calming influence.

Because that's what Danny gave him. Peace. Strange, really, because he thrived on challenge, a fast pace. He understood his life-style was a problem. He would probably end up with a gastric ulcer by forty. Danny made him slow down, think clearer, and gave him a feeling of completion.

Marcus blinked and stretched. Danny had rolled onto his side, facing him with one arm slung casually over his stomach. He wanted more of his warm and comforting weight on him.

He turned his head and took a minute to study Danny's face. He looked so young, so peaceful in sleep. Which he was, he supposed. He *was* young, though twenty-one was a good age. It was the beginning of adulthood, really.

Was he really going to do this? Start a *real* relationship with Sienna's younger brother?

Well, why not? He wouldn't hurt Danny and by most people's standards, he was a good catch. Good looking, successful, financially secure and, he hoped, a pretty good guy.

A tightening in his chest made his breath falter. He had only been in a couple of proper relationships and they had been difficult enough with guys who knew who they were and embraced their sexuality. What would his life be like with someone who wasn't out to his friends and family? Hell, probably. He remembered the lying and sneaking around he did before he told those closest to him. It wasn't a fun time.

Danny moved his hand and shuffled closer, his warm body and affectionate nature making him hug him tighter.

Who was he kidding? He hadn't said *no* to being with Danny. No matter if he was openly out or not, Danny was just discovering his sexuality and that was sexy as hell. The innocent happiness of a single touch was evident in every smile and gasp Danny made. To know he had been the only person to give him the sort of pleasure he needed made him protective. Possessive, even. The very idea that Danny would go off into the world and be picked up by another top made his jaw clench.

He pushed Danny gently onto his back, pulling the covers away as he slid down the younger man's lightly muscled body.

He had such a nice dick. Big head, long shaft, not too thick or purple. Beautiful, really, and swollen with a morning hard-on. *How perfect.*

His hand wrapped around the shaft as if of its own accord and he slipped the head into his mouth.

Why he liked doing this for Danny and had never liked performing oral sex with anyone else, he didn't know. Perhaps it was because he was so untouched. Maybe he needed to please him and make the session good for his young lover. Either way, his cock stretched out to a full erection as he began to move up and down on him and Danny's hand slid into his hair.

"Marcus..." Danny's sleepy voice, so certain about who was giving him pleasure and yet strained with arousal, was the most welcome sound in the world.

Marcus moved his hand and mouth a little faster, enjoying the paradox of soft skin and hard flesh in his mouth. He waited for a loud moan from Danny and when he heard the sound he wanted, he cupped Danny's tight balls and withdrew. His lover moaned again as he moved back up the bed, kissing Danny's abdomen as he went.

"Good morning." He smiled down at his blue-eyed lover, happiness zinging through his veins as his eyes roamed over the smiling face beneath him.

Danny laughed, his eyes sparkling, and wrapped his arms around Marcus' neck.

"It certainly is."

Marcus rubbed his hard cock against his lover's and Danny pulled him down for a scorching kiss. Tongues tangled, moans erupted. He needed him. Now.

He rolled off the bed for condoms and lube, ripping a foil package from the box and tearing it open. This was going to be an awesome ride.

"Can I fuck you?" Danny's question made Marcus jump and he turned back towards the bed, condom in hand.

You're kidding me?

How could he handle a question like that? Honesty would probably be best, but how could he explain such a thing? "Ah, I don't usually do that."

He didn't. It had been years since he'd allowed someone to top him, and it hadn't been pleasant. Of course, those men had been older and bigger, nothing like Danny.

Danny smiled and his eyes twinkled as he rolled off the bed, obviously not deterred in the least. He reached out and took the condom from Marcus' hand.

What are you doing?

"I love it when you fuck me, but can I have a go?"

Ah, I'd prefer you didn't.

He handed over the condom reluctantly, a hysterical laugh caught in his throat. Perhaps he should offer at least once to be fair, since he expected Danny to bottom for him, but he had been looking forward to fucking his young lover again.

"You make sex sound like a ride."

Danny tore the condom open and rolled it on with ease.

"It is."

Fighting his impulse to argue with Danny to get his own way, he lay down on his stomach, his ass on the edge of the bed. *This is going to hurt.*

"Lots of lube, Danny," Marcus said, biting his lip in an attempt not to take it back and jump up and away from his lover.

Danny's lubricated fingers moved over his ass crack and he yelped. Surprise and fear mingled in the hot wave flowing over him.

"How are you going to pull yourself to come like that, Marcus?" Danny asked, his fingers gently exploring Marcus' crevice.

Marcus groaned and crawled up onto his hands and knees, centering himself in the middle of the mattress. Did he really have to? "I was just going to wait until you came and then fuck you."

Danny knelt behind him, the warmth of his hands and thighs welcome. Marcus pushed back against him subconsciously and Danny caressed his legs a little more.

He took a shuddering breath. Danny was gentle, passionate and giving. Maybe this would be different to anything else he'd experienced.

"If you really don't want this, I won't make you." Danny's voice was as soothing as his gentle hands were on Marcus's thighs.

Marcus groaned again in frustration and relaxed. He was being unfair and ruining a moment that should be enjoyable for them both.

"No, I want to. You deserve to know what both sides feel like. Just go slow."

Marcus dropped his head and waited, dreading the burn and the feeling of powerlessness this gave him. There was a reason he always topped, and this was it. He didn't like to feel out of control or to give the dominant role to another. Didn't like it at work, didn't want it in bed. It may have made him seem like a control freak, but it worked for him.

Much to Marcus' surprise, Danny didn't thrust in right away. He ran his hands up and down his back in a caress so sweet it made him moan. The foreplay was so unexpected his muscles relax even more.

"I won't hurt you, you know. I just want to show you how good this feels when you do it to me."

Marcus' heart ached as Danny's voiced rolled over him. If this was going to be a real relationship then he needed to trust Danny on all levels, starting from right here.

Danny moved his warm hands between his legs and caressed his balls before pushing two well-lubricated fingers into his ass.

Marcus let out soft sigh as his body hummed. Burning pain shot through his ass, the combination of possession and passion making his breath catch and his body relax. The pain soon melted into a sizzling pleasure, shooting his arousal to a new high. *Thank God.*

Danny slid his fingers in and out, stretching, stroking, easing the way for penetration. Relief and gratitude filled him and his balls tightened. "I'm supposed to be helping make this easy for you, not the other way around."

He groaned again as Danny slipped a hot hand beneath him and stroked his cock a few times while still fingering him.

Danny chuckled, removed his inquisitive fingers and pressed his cock to Marcus' entrance. "We can learn together."

The importance and magnitude of that statement wasn't lost on

Marcus, but as Danny thrust into the hilt in one powerful shove, his brain shut down like a lid on a jar.

"Fuucckkk." He couldn't believe how amazing it felt. Pure pleasure was centering in his belly and pulsing out in waves. He tilted his pelvis up to feel that blissful contact with his prostate and began to rock against his lover. "Oh my God, that feels amazing."

How is he doing that? Wow.

Danny moved back then thrust back again slowly, causing pleasure to ripple along Marcus's cock. His lover found his rhythm and began sliding in and out of Marcus as though they had all day. The care Danny was taking making his heart clench with love for him.

Oh, shit. I fucking love him. Damn...

"Aw, fuck."

Marcus dropped his shoulders down closer to the mattress and ran his hands through his hair as he let his head fall forward. He closed his eyelids. Splinters of light pierced his vision, and sizzling sensations flowed over his whole body.

The more Danny fucked him, the more pleasure it gave him, and he questioned why he hadn't liked this before. What made this so different? Maybe it was the care and patience Danny was showing him. All of the other men had been big guys who felt they had to master him. Hurt him. Dominate. Danny wasn't doing that. Danny was loving him.

"You're so tight around me. Am I hurting you?" Danny asked, moving his hand up and down Marcus' back in a reassuring way.

Marcus' cock grew thick, swollen, and throbbed to come. He didn't think he even had to touch it. He was sure he could come from the penetration alone. How amazing was that?

"Go faster, Danny," he urged his lover, needing more.

Now given permission, Danny gripped Marcus' hips and thrust harder and faster. Danny was gasping and groaning above him, and their sweaty skin slapped together in that "fuck" sound he loved so much. It still wasn't enough.

"Danny, please. More." Marcus heard his words and couldn't believe they had come out of his mouth. When had he ever begged? For anything?

"I want you to come too, Marcus," Danny panted, his voice strained as he held onto his control better than any man Marcus had ever been with.

Marcus groaned. He didn't want to move in case the pleasure changed. But Danny wanted him to touch himself, so he dropped his chest onto the bed and reached for his cock. His balls tightened instantly, and tingles of pleasure ran down the backs of his legs. "Ah... I'm coming, Danny. Harder!"

Marcus roared, his face pressed into the sheet as Danny fucked him with abandon. His orgasm gathered and tore him apart from the inside. His seed pulsed out of him, white lights flashing behind his closed eyelids as the spasms went on and on, rippling through his body. Danny gripped his hips hard and thrust one more time, his spasming cock hot inside him.

When Danny pulled out slowly, Marcus collapsed onto his side, panting, sweat dripping down his back. Danny disappeared for a moment before returning to spoon him from behind and slip a hand around his waist.

"Thank you for that," Danny whispered against his ear, kissing him then lying back down.

Marcus forced himself to roll over and look at his lover, lethargy threatening to drag him back down to sleep. He should be thanking Danny for showing him the difference.

"How was it for you?" He had to know. The sex had been great, but he still had a preference.

Danny smiled and kissed him, his lips soft and tender.

"It was really good, but I think I prefer it the other way."

Marcus laughed and rolled on top of Danny again. Relief and happiness coursed through him like fluttering wings, sending white energy through his whole body.

"Thank God. I couldn't give up that role completely. Though, occasionally, I don't mind if you wanna swap."

Danny reached up and ruffled Marcus' hair in an endearing way.

"So, you want to keep doing this? Seeing me?"

Once again Danny surprised him, and he felt his eyebrows rise. Every time he thought he had Danny pegged, he shocked him anew. Danny was sensitive, passionate, honest, and as ballsy as all get-out. Amazing.

"Definitely. Though I don't want to hide in here forever."

Danny nodded, his eyes guarded as he glanced away.

"We can go out. I just don't want to tell my friends and family yet."

Marcus smiled and kissed his lover on the mouth again, not liking the sudden change of atmosphere. "Fair enough. Let's just take it one step at a time, then."

Chapter Eight

DANNY STOOD OUTSIDE MARCUS' work, waiting for him to finish while watching the city life go by. They had been dating for six months but he still got excited flutters in his belly whenever he was about to see his lover.

He was even more enthusiastic that normal because he hadn't seen Marcus in over a week. They'd had a big fight last Saturday and hadn't talked much since.

Danny closed his eyes and relived the conversation.

Marcus stood in his kitchen, hands on his lean hips.

"I want you to come to my friend's thirtieth, Danny."

He wrung his hands and cleared his throat. "You know I have to go to my mate's twenty-first."

Marcus groaned.

"Why? And why can't I come with you? We've been seeing each other for six fucking months, Danny!"

Danny stood up, wanting to leave.

"Don't you dare leave! We need to talk about this."

Danny turned and eyed his lover. "You're yelling at me, not talking."

Marcus took a huge breath and placed his hands on the kitchen bench.

"Are you putting it off because you still aren't sure about who you are?"

Danny shook his head. That was the least of his problems. "No, I'm gay, Marcus. I know I am. But my friends shouldn't have to deal with my thirty-year-old lover. It's not fair to put that on them, they'd be uncomfortable, not mention have a fucking fit!"

"What the hell's wrong with me?"

"Nothing, Marcus. Please. I love being with you, but I just can't. Not yet."

He walked over to Marcus, who was positively shaking with anger. "I hate this. I want you in my life. At my side. I want you to come meet my parents, Danny!"

"I know." Danny soothed, touching and kissing his lover, as much of a distraction as it was a reward to Marcus for allowing him this extra time.

Danny shook his head and opened his eyes. Although he'd diffused the situation the best way he could, things were strained between them. He'd wanted to call every night but hadn't been sure what to say. Marcus wanted something from him that he just couldn't give yet.

Nothing in his life was going to end well unless he got the courage to come out to his friends or family. Marcus wanted him to be a real part of his life and he'd been just plain scared.

Scared he would enjoy the new beginning more than his old life. Afraid he would get caught and have to face the reality that some of his past friends may not want to see him again.

But where could he and Marcus go from here anyway?

"Hey, babe," Marcus called as he walked out the front door of the skyscraper he called work, his hand already going to the knot in his tie, pulling it down.

Danny couldn't help the smile that spread across his face. His lover was gorgeous. In a suit, in the buff, even in a pair of cargos and a pink t-shirt, he made his gut flip flop.

"Hi." He stepped up and Marcus's arms went around him in a brief but intense hug. It was their compromise on public displays of affection.

"Night, Marcus. Hey, Danny," Dave called, waving his hand.

Dave was one of the straight guys from Friday night football. He was kind of cool.

"Hey, Dave." Danny waved and watched a cute little blonde woman walk up and smile in their direction.

"Hey, Marcus, is this the boyfriend you're always talking about?"

Marcus coughed next to him and Danny stiffened, waiting on his lover's reply.

"Yeah, sort of. Danny this is Gabby. Gabby this is Danny."

Gabby held her hand out and Danny shook it, interested to hear what else the cute blonde would say about his boyfriend. "What's Marcus been saying about me?"

"Not much." Gabby grinned. "We've all been quizzing him because he always looks so happy now. What have you been doing to him?"

Danny's horny mind conjured up images of Marcus fucking him in front of the mirror, and he couldn't stop the blush that spread across his face. "We watch football and eat, mostly."

Gabby giggled and looked at Marcus. "Yep, he's great. Make sure you come to our Christmas party, Danny. It's about time Marcus brought someone."

Danny nodded and stepped closer to his lover, the wall of warmth comforting as always.

Gabby waved and headed off.

"Let's get out of here before you attract any more attention." Marcus waggled his eyebrows at Danny, grabbed his hand and tugged him toward the car park.

"Do you tell people you have a boyfriend?" Danny asked, unable to keep his interest quiet. They'd never really discussed how they saw each other, and except for one brief conversation about being "exclusive," they didn't really touch on the subject past that.

Marcus shrugged his broad shoulders and opened the car.

"If they ask, I do. Why?" He looked straight at Danny, his eyes daring him to argue the point.

Danny swallowed, torn between the part of him that loved how Marcus was proud to be with him, and the other half that felt guilty that he couldn't return that level of commitment. None of him wanted to refute the statement. They were definitely an item. "No reason, I've just never heard you say it."

They climbed into Marcus's top-of-the-line Mercedes and Danny instantly reached for Marcus' thigh, the muscles tight beneath his palm.

"Well, I don't get the chance. We don't go out and meet anyone."

Danny could hear the bitterness behind the words and bit his tongue to stop from snapping back. Marcus knew why he couldn't do that yet, so why was it always brought up?

"I've really missed you this week."

The frown marring Marcus' brow smoothed out as his face relaxed.

"Good. Then you're coming home with me tonight?"

A lump rose in Danny's throat. He hadn't looked forward to explaining his reasons to Marcus. "I can't. I have early classes and my parents have been noticing how often I'm not sleeping at home. They want to know where I'm going all the time."

Marcus groaned in obvious frustration and moved Danny's hand up to his groin and pressed down.

Oh, yeah.

He stroked Marcus' cock head through his pants and moved his finger up and down the length. Marcus' dick was hard and getting harder under his touch.

Danny gasped and his own body quickened. "Will you drive me home?"

Marcus eyed him, brows drawn down.

"Aren't your parents home?"

Danny shook his head and rubbed along the length of Marcus' cock. "No, they've gone out for dinner. Please. Come home with me."

Danny could see his lover's indecision in his shadowed eyes and straight lips. Begging was in order. "Please, baby, please..."

Marcus groaned again and his hands clenched around the steering wheel.

"Fine, but we need to talk about this, Danny."

Danny withdrew his hand and stared out the window so Marcus couldn't see his grin.

They drove home in silence, the air between them hot and electric with anticipation.

Chapter Nine

"NO ONE'S HOME FOR the next few hours." Danny grinned at him as he unlocked the front door to his parents' house.

Marcus suppressed the urge to groan again with his lover's need to hide their relationship from his parents. The situation annoyed the hell out of him. "You know I'm too old for this, don't you?"

Danny pushed open the heavy wooden front door and grabbed his shirt, hauling him inside. Marcus loved how enthusiastic he was with him now.

"What? Too old to fuck me in my parents' house?" Danny pulled him into the living room and began undoing the buttons on his white work shirt.

A growl erupted from Marcus' chest as he grabbed Danny's hands and pinned him against the wall. His boy loved things a little rough and he was in the mood to give it to him.

"I'll fuck you in the middle of town in front of everyone. You know that's not what I mean."

Danny's excited face dimmed, and Marcus felt a stab of regret. He shouldn't have brought it up again, especially now.

"You know I want to be with you Marcus. I just don't know how to tell anyone."

Marcus sighed and rested his head against Danny's forehead for a moment. He would do anything for this man, even if it meant living in the shadows for a while longer. He dropped a kiss onto Danny's lips and whispered into his ear.

"You know I'll wait for you to be ready. I just hate not being able to be with you all the time and I don't like going a whole week without seeing you."

He ground his erection into his lover. It had been a very frustrating week.

Marcus groaned, reached around his body and squeezed his ass.

"I've missed you too, Marcus."

Marcus moaned and grabbed hold of Danny's face, kissing him with all the pent-up passion of a long, lonely week.

"What the fuck are you doing, Marcus?" Sienna's voice ricocheted throughout the small room with the force of a cannon firing.

Marcus stilled, his muscles freezing as shock rippled through him with the effect of a boulder being dropped into a still pond. *Fuck!* He had no idea she would be home and judging by the look on Danny's face, neither did he.

"It's okay, Sienna," Danny explained as he stepped around Marcus and moved closer to his sister.

Sienna stared him down, her blue eyes glittering and anger radiating off her in waves. Marcus could almost see them as though they were a tangible thing, and it changed the temperature in the room from boiling to ice.

"Danny, could you leave Marcus and me alone please?"

Danny shook his head, anger present in his clenched jaw and fists.

"No. Marcus hasn't done anything wrong."

This argument wasn't going to get them anywhere, sibling love would win out and he didn't want to get into the fight. He moved next to Danny and smiled at him. He needed to talk to Sienna, and he preferred she take her anger out on him instead of Danny. "Give us ten minutes alone, babe?"

He heard Sienna's shocked gasp but didn't let it affect him as he gently kissed Danny on the lips and tilted his head toward the door.

Danny looked between them, his split allegiance obvious. Marcus tried his best to smile with confidence, but she worried him. This could get very messy quickly and he had no idea how it was going to affect his relationship with Danny. A relationship he had come to put at the top of his priorities.

"Okay, I'll get us some drinks."

Danny slowly moved to the door, glancing back once more while biting his bottom lip, then left.

Slap!

Sienna's hand cracked against his cheek hard, the sound reverberating in his head and sending his head flying sideways.

"You're fucking my baby brother?" Sienna spat at him.

Lights exploded behind Marcus' eye and pain spread throughout his face.

"Ow," he complained, cradling his jaw with his hand and looking back at his friend.

"You didn't need to do that, Sienna."

She stomped her foot and her hands clenched into fists at her sides.

"You didn't answer my question."

Marcus felt his mouth turn up at the ends. "Was that a question?"

The look of horror Sienna gave him was truly heartbreaking. Her mouth dropped open and her eyes were absolutely devastated. He had always thought she had been fine, comfortable with him being gay. Obviously, his sexuality came into question when her brother was involved.

"How could you, Marcus?"

Marcus clenched his jaw and tried to relax the muscles. Getting mad would not solve anything. He needed to be honest. "How could I what, Sienna? Fall in love with your brother?"

Sienna's eyes widened comically, and Marcus heard a gasp from the hallway. *Damn.*

He hadn't told Danny how he felt yet. What a way to find out.

Sienna was still looking horrified, but her eyes had softened now as she looked at him. He knew Danny was watching but tried his hardest to concentrate on his friend instead.

"Look, Sienna, I'm sorry if this is a shock to you, but I do, and I think he feels the same way. He makes me happy and I would never hurt him. Can you live with that?"

Sienna shook her head in slow motion, biting her lip as tears swam in her pretty blue eyes. His chest squeezed tight as his heart sank.

"My parents, Marcus..."

Marcus sighed and rubbed both hands over his face. *I am so over this sort of shit.* He loved Danny, but this was the reason he never dated guys in the closet. It didn't matter how hard he tried, how good a person and lover he was, he'd never be fully accepted for who he was. He deserved better than this. "I'll go."

Sienna nodded and didn't say a word to stop him, which probably hurt more than the physical slap to his face.

Marcus walked out of the living room and found Danny there, his back pressed up against the wall.

"You meant what you said?"

Marcus nodded, though reluctant to discuss it considering their audience. "You need to talk to your sister, but call me later, okay?"

Danny nodded, his eyes shimmering with unshed tears. He was so beautiful. His perfect angel. He couldn't resist reassuring his lover once more despite his own twisting gut. He bent forward, cupped

Danny's jaw and pressed his lips as carefully as he could down on them.

Danny moaned against his lips and Marcus broke away, looking deep into Danny's blue eyes. "Call me."

Danny nodded and Marcus left, a heavy weight gripping his heart.

Chapter Ten

OVERWHELMED YET TOTALLY ECSTATIC, Danny let his head fall back against the plaster wall and his eyes slid shut. *Marcus loves me.* The pleasure of that information vibrated through every cell, making it difficult to contain a sob.

"Danny," Sienna's voice cut through the protective ring of happiness and dragged him back into reality. *Crap.*

He opened his eyes and stared into his sister's blue irises, identical to his own. The world came crashing down with the force of a bucket of cold water on his head. Reality sucked. "You shouldn't have done that, Sienna."

Sienna crossed her arms defensively over her body and straightened her spine.

Danny pushed away from the wall, ready to leave. He didn't want to have this conversation. Not with Sienna, not with anyone.

"What are you going to tell Mum and Dad?" Sienna's voice stalled him when he reached the end of the room.

Danny twisted back around to face his sister. "I'm not telling Mum and Dad anything at the moment."

Sienna turned her head away and a heavy weight landed into Danny's stomach.

He gasped. "You wouldn't!"

She dropped her hands and shrugged.

"I have to Danny. This is too important."

Danny clenched his fists, fear and anger mingling to make one hell of an intense emotion. "It's none of your fucking business, Sienna! I've been seeing Marcus for six months. I love him, he loves me. We don't need to bring Mum and Dad into this."

Sienna gasped, a hand flying to her mouth.

"You've kept it to yourself that long?"

Danny groaned and ran a shaking hand through his hair. This was spiraling out of his control, slipping through his fingers like running water. "Look, I'll tell them. I will. I just don't know how."

Sienna took the few steps over to him and reached out a hand. Danny took it and squeezed the offered sibling support.

"You know you have to tell them. As long as you're sure it's not just a passing phase?"

The hope in Sienna's voice and the way her eyes lit up, made Danny drop her hand like it was red-hot. He clenched his teeth and flared his nostrils, then took a deep breath to calm himself. "This is who I am, Sienna. I can't change who I am or who I love."

Sienna took a step back, her arms wrapping protectively around her body once again and her face turning passive.

"Well, baby brother, you better be sure about this, because the shit is about to hit the fan."

Danny turned and ran upstairs, slamming the door and locking it behind him. He had to tell his parents now. She had backed him into a corner. If he didn't then his sister would, and he couldn't have that.

He threw himself face down onto the pillow and wrapped his arms around it. *Fuck, Marcus. I need you... Where are you?*

. . .

Danny heard his parents arrive home hours later, their voices ringing through the big house, but he couldn't bring himself to open the door to greet them. Sienna wouldn't still be there, surely. He had a little more time.

There was a knock at his door.

"Danny, can we come in?"

Oh, fuck! No, sister, you didn't!

"Sure, Mum," Danny called out as he got to his feet and staggered to the door. His knees were weak and his gut tight.

He unlocked the door with trembling fingers and slid back onto the bed.

Both his mum and his dad walked in.

"Hey, what's up?" he asked them, already noting the strained looks on their faces, the pinched tightness around their mouths.

His mother sat on the chair opposite him and his dad leaned against the wall.

Danny's mother spoke first.

"We, uh, just had a talk with Sienna downstairs and she thought we should have a chat."

Danny nodded, swallowing hard as bile rose up. *Oh my God. This is it.*

"Do you have anything to tell us, Danny?"

Danny glanced between his mum and dad. His dad wouldn't look him in the eye, he just stared at the carpet. His mum was biting her lip and twirling her fingers.

He had to tell them. They already knew, but he had to say the words, *I'm gay.* Those two simple words had spun round his head so much in the past six months, they no longer seemed like real words.

Marcus. This is for Marcus, he thought. *And for you*, a small voice inside reminded him.

Danny sat up straighter. "Yes. As I'm sure Sienna has already told you, I'm in love with Marcus."

Danny's dad pushed away from the wall and began pacing.

"That's impossible, Danny. No one in our family is gay. You can't be."

Danny tried to hide his smile but knew he had failed when his dad turned to glare at him. "That's not exactly the best response, Dad."

His dad glared at him harder and continued to pace.

His mum moved forward on her chair and smiled at him.

"Danny, please. Tell us it's a mistake. I mean, you can't really choose to be gay. You'll never have a family. Your life is going to be so much more difficult this way. Please, Danny."

His mum's pleading blue eyes caused tears to well in his own.

"It isn't a choice, Mum." His voice cracked and he cleared his throat. "I've known for a few years that I didn't really like any of the girls I'd dated, but it wasn't until I met Marcus that I *really* knew."

"I am going to kill that kid." His dad's furious voice made Danny stand up, his own fists clenched on either side of him.

"You will not. I fell in love with Marcus. He hasn't done anything wrong except love me back."

His dad made a disgusted noise and strode over to the door.

He opened it and stared back at Danny.

"We will not support this lifestyle, Danny. If you want this, then you need to get out. I won't have a queer son living under my roof."

The look of hurt and disgust his dad threw him as he stormed out of the room was enough to knock the wind right out of Danny. He fell back onto the bed, his throat constricting so that he gagged in an attempt to breathe.

"He c-can't m-mean that," Danny gasped to draw breath.

His mum stood up and moved toward the door too.

"We taught you that you can do anything you want, Danny. Achieve any goal you set your mind to. But we can't support you in this."

And with that lethal blow, his mother also left him alone, leaving his heart in shreds. His parents, the two people who were meant to support him, love him for all time, had broken him. Tears overflowed and sobs forced their way out of his throat. What the hell was he going to do now?

Chapter Eleven

DANNY DIDN'T CALL HIM. Not that night, not the next day, nor the following. The wait was horrible. Marcus had never been so out of control of a situation and he agonized every minute over what to do.

Every relationship he had been in, he had ended it. Every goal at work he set himself, he achieved. But this thing with Danny had made him helpless.

Over and over, Marcus picked up his mobile. His thumb was getting sprained from checking his messages. No text, no e-mail. Nothing. He had never been one of those people glued to their phone with no real concept of how rude it was. Until now.

Is Danny okay? Maybe I should just call?

No! He had told Danny to call him. Twice, if he remembered correctly. It hurt a lot to think that someone he loved had rejected him. Much worse than he had expected it to. The rejection—the silence—was like an elephant sitting on his chest 24/7.

When Marcus lay in bed at night, he could almost feel Danny beside him. His warmth, his breath. Danny's giving nature, in and out of bed. See that crazily beautiful smile and hear cheeky laugh. All those little things that had brought happiness into his life, peace to his heart.

He must be going crazy. Worse, he'd started to act like Dr. Jekyll and Mr. Hyde. He alternated between, *Fuck him! How can he do this to me?* and *Oh my God, I hope he's all right.* He had no peace from the constant struggle inside his own head.

A knock sounded at the door and Marcus glanced at the clock on the wall. Nine in the evening on a Tuesday. Who would that be?

He swung open the door to see his lover standing before him.

Marcus stared and stood frozen, shock warring with relief that he was finally here. Danny wore old jeans, a crumpled white t-shirt, and his hair was sticking out at all odd angles. He looked worse than someone who had been dragged over a hedge backward.

"What are you doing here?"

Danny shrugged and shifted his weight, as though exhausted and not able to stand still.

"Can I come in?"

Marcus stood back and waved him in. "Of course, you can, I just expected you to call."

They walked into the kitchen and Marcus pulled two beers out of the fridge on autopilot. A hundred questions raced through his head. He opened both bottles and handed one to the man he wanted to be his partner in life. A man he had not spoken to for two days, which felt like two lifetimes.

He had only one important question. "So, what happened?"

Danny chugged down half the beer then collapsed into the chair.

"My parents kicked me out."

Shock waves rippled through Marcus, rendering him almost speechless. He blinked a couple of times, then swallowed hard to force his vocal cords to work. "They... what?"

Danny smiled his nervous, lopsided smile.

"They told me that I couldn't be gay and still live at home. I waited, hoping they would change their minds. When they didn't, I realized I can't stop loving you. So, I left."

Marcus heard so much in those few sentences that he couldn't comprehend all of the information in real time. He shook his head to clear the confusion.

"You left... and you love me?" His voice croaked as his heart soared with happiness.

Danny nodded and Marcus rounded the bench to take his lover into his arms, crushing the smaller body against him. "You shouldn't have to give up your family for me."

Danny kissed him intensely on the lips before pulling back.

"It wasn't just for you, I did it for me. This is who I am, and you are what I need."

Marcus's breath caught in his throat and he coughed to clear it as he glanced away. Danny completely unmanned him with his simple truth. He never played any games, he was just who he was. He took his breath away.

"So, last week we were fighting over not being able to go to a party together and now I'm asking you to move in with me? What a week."

Danny laughed and kissed him.

"Was that a question?"

Marcus swallowed the lump in his throat. He didn't like the way such an important question had come about, but this was what he needed. He had wanted to ask him months ago, but it hadn't been possible. Danny was still at university and his parents would have been suspicious. Now, it seemed, the door had been opened. "Move in with me. Be my partner in every sense of the word."

Unshed tears swam in Danny's eyes as he nodded.

"Yeah, I'd love that."

He finally stepped away and took Marcus's hand.

"All my stuff is in my car downstairs. But before we bring it all up, I need you to finish what we started a couple of days ago."

Marcus saw so much heat in Danny's eyes, he stumbled as they moved toward his bedroom. Their bedroom, now. "Horny, are you?"

Danny shook his head and stepped into the bedroom, his blue eyes shining with happiness.

"No, I'm in love."

Marcus stepped up to his brave, beautiful man and dragged off Danny's clothes. T-shirt, jeans and jocks were all gone in seconds.

Danny returned the favor, stripping Marcus' clothes in between heated kisses and touches. Their need for each other was urgent, but there was something more at that moment. A desperation coupled with an intense passion he had never experienced before.

Naked, Marcus stared at his lover's quivering, erect cock. He took a step forward to touch and kiss it. He had missed Danny so much.

Instead, Danny shocked him by dropping to his knees and reaching for him.

"What are you doing?" It was an inane question. The object of Danny's concentration was obvious, yet he couldn't believe his eyes.

"I'm going to suck your cock, if that's all right?" Danny gazed up at him, his sarcasm not lost considering the cheekiness of his smile. The erotic words weren't lost on Marcus either. His cock thickened and jutted out proudly.

He threaded his fingers into Danny's blond hair and guided him gently toward his aching body. Danny opened his mouth and sucked all of his aching cock head in. Teeth grazed his shaft and the pressure was too intense.

Marcus gasped and tightened his hold on Danny's hair. "Ah, a bit gentler, baby."

Danny came off him with a wet pop and gazed up, his eyes fearful.

"I'm sorry."

Marcus laughed and shook his head. "Don't be. I've been waiting for this for six months." He pushed on Danny's head and Danny wrapped his lips around him again. Wet heat enveloped him.

"Use your hand and just tongue the end," Marcus managed to get out as pleasure tingled along his legs. It had been so long since he'd felt this good.

Danny moved his hand and his warm mouth faster, Marcus' balls tightening in response. Unable to stand the intense delight a moment longer, he stepped back, grabbed Danny's hand, and pulled him to his feet.

"That bad?" Danny's eyes appeared wounded. Marcus groaned and wrapped his arms around his lover. Their cocks pressed against their stomachs, the feeling of heat and arousal intoxicating.

"No. So good I was about to come down your throat."

Danny smiled and kissed him.

"I wouldn't mind."

He cupped Danny's jaw and kissed him slowly, exploring the inner recesses of his mouth. Half of him wanted this moment to last forever, but his need was too great.

His balls tight, he reached down and gave Danny's cock a few long tugs. Danny moaned against his mouth and thrust his hips in time with his slow caress.

Yes, they were both too horny to wait any longer.

He broke off and went straight for the condoms in the side drawer. "I need to come inside you, Danny."

Danny nodded and strode over for the lube.

"On your back, Marcus."

Marcus gaped. What had got into his lover tonight? Danny had never gone down on him before and Marcus had never complained about the lack of it. He had expected that when Danny was truly comfortable, it would all come together naturally.

But what was this? Was his lover trying to top again?

Marcus climbed onto the bed and rolled onto his back. "I can bottom later, Danny, if you need that."

He didn't really want to, but anything to keep his lover happy at the moment.

Danny climbed onto the bed and rolled the condom on to Marcus' shaft. Marcus' breath hissed out between his lips. The pressure so fantastic and his confirmation that Danny *didn't* want to top was brilliant.

Danny swung his leg over Marcus's waist and applied lube to his hole. Marcus's belly tightened with a mixture of fear and happiness. Danny loved him and wanted him still.

Amazing.

"I don't need to top. I just wanted to try something different."

Danny positioned Marcus' cock at his slick entrance. Marcus groaned as Danny squeezed him and grabbed a hold of his hips. This confidence from his lover was awesome.

"You *are* topping, my love. You're in control. Ride me." Marcus pulled Danny down and thrust his hips up, groaning as his cock head became encased in hot flesh. Danny gasped and pressed all the way down.

Marcus arched and threw his head back. "Oh my God, I have missed you so much."

Danny began to move up and down, his hands on either side of Marcus' head as he rode hard.

"I love you, Marcus."

Marcus opened his eyes and glanced up into twin sapphires of trust and love. The two things that a real relationship should be based on. It was the only way they would survive.

"And I love you." He moved one of his hands to Danny's hard cock, stroking fast.

Danny moaned and moved faster, riding him like he'd done it a thousand times before.

Marcus' balls tightened and he thrust up when Danny moved down, bending his knees up so he could put his feet on the mattress and use all his strength.

"Oh, fuck, yes. Marcus!" Danny moved faster, thrusting down harder, his fine body covered in a thin film of sweat.

"I'm coming!" Marcus roared as his balls exploded, shooting his seed, pleasurable tingles spreading through his legs and up through his body.

Danny rode him right through, gasping and panting. His face was red, his eyes glazed over. Marcus tightened his hold on Danny's cock and pumped him fast. Danny jerked, his spine arching as he came.

"Oh, fuck..."

Hot, white fluid spurted out of Danny, all over Marcus' hand and chest. He watched his lover's face the whole time, enjoying every little spasm and groan until Danny slumped forward.

He slipped from Danny's body and pulled his lover down to his chest, not caring about the mess for the moment. "You know I'll look after you, Danny."

Danny snuggled in and sighed.

"We'll look after each other, Marcus."

Marcus smiled and kissed the top of Danny's head. He had found the perfect partner.

His lover groaned and pushed himself up again.

"Starting with a shower?"

Marcus laughed, his head light with happiness. Some way, somehow, he had found what he had been looking for. "No argument here."

They climbed off the bed and ran to the shower together, their laughter filling the air. Life would not always be easy, but he had confidence in their love for one another. Everything else would sort itself out with time.

Epilogue

A month later

"THIS IS A BIT FANCY, Marcus. You know you don't need to spoil me." Danny grinned at his lover as he was gently led into an expensive restaurant at Crown Casino.

"It's your graduation present."

Danny laughed. "I don't even know *if* I'm graduating yet. I haven't got my results."

Marcus scoffed, as he always did when Danny doubted himself.

"I bet you get an average of distinction." Marcus turned to the maître d'. "Reservation for Anderson." The older man looked at the book then indicated they should follow.

"What do you bet me, Marcus?" Danny asked, sliding his hand into his lover's. Aware of other people's sensitivities but no longer afraid to show affection toward Marcus in public, he'd even gotten into a fight a time or two when people called them inappropriate. Times were changing, and the laws had followed suit. He planned to stand up and scream his love to the world when it was time.

Marcus stopped their progress through the restaurant and whispered into his ear.

"If you get the score I expect, you are coming with me for a month in Europe."

Danny frowned. He didn't like taking Marcus's money. "That's hardly a punishment."

Marcus grinned.

"And if you don't, I'll give you a night of no-holds-barred sex."

Danny laughed. "Don't we do that already?"

Marcus turned and nodded at the man they were meant to be following.

"I'll do anything you want. You can choose."

Ideas began to fill Danny's head and his unruly body twitched in response. "Anything?" he asked, grinning at his lover.

Marcus swallowed and he looked slightly nervous now.

"Yes, anything."

Danny laughed at his Marcus' discomfort. There were a few bondage scenarios he would *love* to try. "Keep walking. He's waiting for us."

Marcus nodded, but didn't move, pulling Danny even closer.

"You know I love you more than anything?"

Danny nodded, a sick feeling beginning to burn in his stomach. "Yes, of course I do."

Marcus nodded once more and pulled him the ten meters to the booth that the waiter was indicating.

Danny stepped up beside his lover and stared straight into the eyes of his parents. His mouth hung open in shock and he turned to glare at his boyfriend. "You set this up?"

Marcus tilted his head.

"Have a seat, Danny."

His jaw set hard, yet much happier to see his parents than he ever thought possible, he sat down.

"Hi, Danny." His mum smiled and reached out a hand to him.

Danny allowed her to touch the back of his hand, but it soon felt too forced and he brought it back into his lap. No, that wasn't right either. He dropped it down onto Marcus' thigh, where his hand always rested, and watched his parents.

That's better.

Danny's mother blushed and his father picked up his water glass and drank half of it in one gulp. They were still sitting, though.

"Danny, I rang your parents to see if they wanted to join us for a celebratory dinner."

Danny smiled sweetly at his boyfriend. "How nice of you, Marcus."

Marcus elbowed him in the ribs and Danny let out an "Ow," before he forced his gaze back to his parents.

"Danny, we are so sorry. We honestly didn't realize that you were so serious. I mean..." His mum stopped and looked at her husband for support.

Danny's dad placed his glass down and looked directly into Danny's eyes. "We shouldn't have asked you to leave."

"No, you shouldn't have."

That got him another elbow to his ribs, and he squeezed Marcus's thigh hard. "Would you quit doing that?"

Marcus glared at him.

"It took my parents two years to speak to me after I came out. You know this. Cut your mum and dad some slack, would you?"

Danny huffed a few times then forced himself to calm down. They were here, and that was a huge statement in itself. "I don't want to move back home."

Danny's parents shared worried glances.

"Yes, Marcus said as much. We just wanted to hear it from you."

Danny gazed up at his boyfriend and noticed the tense set of his jaw. "You weren't worried... were you, Marcus?"

Marcus turned to look at him, his eyes shining with all the love and honesty Danny had come to expect from him.

"I hoped you wouldn't want to, but I can't make you stay if you want to go home, Danny."

Oh God! When would these people get the point?

"Okay, listen, all of you."

All three people turned to stare at him, and Danny mustered all the courage he had only recently discovered he had. "I love Marcus and love living with him. I can't and won't move home. He is my home now. But I would also like to be a part of your lives again. If—" His parents were already nodding, but halted as he raised his voice. "If you accept Marcus as my partner. The same way you do Steve and Sienna."

His parents didn't even look at each other, they both just nodded with jolting motions and it was his dad who spoke first.

"We can do that, Danny."

The waiter arrived and they all picked up their menus to order. Danny settled back into his chair and watched his family. The one he had been born into and the one he had created.

He had followed his heart to find the person he truly needed, and he couldn't be happier. He wouldn't change Marcus for anyone and now his parents seemed to accept who he was, he didn't need to. He winked at Marcus and grinned. The road ahead might be rocky, but they were on the right path. Together.

Tommy's Bear

Chapter One

TOMMY'S best friend approached the table, gorgeous smile in place and his young, blond boy-toy in tow. *Fan-fucking-tastic.* When he had invited Marcus out for a drink, he had hoped his friend would be alone. When had Marcus become one of those guys who couldn't go anywhere without the Mrs.?

"Hey, Tommy." Marcus grinned as he pulled out the barstool and sat down opposite him. Danny, his new, young boyfriend, fell into the chair next to Marcus.

"Hi, Tommy."

Tommy nodded at them both, trying to control his face so that the men wouldn't see how annoyed he was. It wasn't that Danny was a bad kid—well actually he was a very smart, beautiful young man— but on his birthday the last thing Tommy wanted was to watch these two canoodling all night.

Hoping to distract himself from his negative thoughts, he rose from his seat. "Hey boys, what do you want to drink?"

Marcus began to stand. "It's your birthday, Tommy. My treat."

Tommy's eyebrows rose when Danny stood quickly and placed a

hand on Marcus' shoulder, pushing him back down. "I'll get them, babe. Beer?"

"Yes, please."

Danny looked over at him with a raised eyebrow. "Another whiskey, Tommy?"

"Yeah, thanks."

Danny headed off towards the bar, and Marcus twisted around to watch him go before he turned toward Tommy, his lips pulled tight.

"You didn't want me to bring Danny, did you?"

Damn, but Marcus had always been able to read him too well.

Tommy was sure his guilt showed on his face, but he tried his best to fake his way through by feigning surprise. "Don't be stupid. He's your boyfriend. Of course, I figured you'd bring him with you."

Marcus eyed him critically, his mouth still pulled down. Heat rose in Tommy's cheeks and he blundered through a bit more of the conversation. "I admit, I did think it would just be us two, but only because I forget you're shackled now."

He choked out a laugh, trying to make the statement more of a joke, though he knew it fell flat when Marcus looked away.

"Danny's no shackle, mate. He's a blessing."

Marcus looked back up, and Tommy was caught off guard by the passion in his deep brown eyes. He and Marcus had shared two nights together when they had first met, and even in the very midst of things, he'd never seen an expression like that on Marcus' face.

"Yeah, I know, Marcus. I'm..." Tommy sucked in a deep breath and forced the words out. "I'm happy for you."

And he was, mostly. He was also jealous as all hell, as was evidenced by the strained smile currently on his face and the burning in his gut.

A little bit of envy was aimed at Danny for having Marcus—the man he had always kind of wanted—but also because of their love, their happiness. That was the real kicker.

Marcus made an "Uh-huh" sound of disbelief and smiled when Danny returned with their drinks.

"Happy birthday, Tommy."

Tommy picked up the glass Danny had pushed in front of him and lifted it into the air. "Thanks, guys."

They clinked glasses and drank. Tommy hissed as the fine, expensive whiskey slid down his throat. Nice and smooth, even better than the one he'd bought himself. The boy had good taste.

"That's a nice drop, Danny. Thanks."

Danny picked up his own beer and leaned down to kiss Marcus quickly on the lips.

"No problem. I'll see you guys later."

"Thanks, gorgeous."

Tommy furrowed his eyebrows at them both. *Huh?*

Danny strode away and stood at the bar again, tapping his foot against the wooden floor in time with the music. He was a little too cute.

Tommy looked back at his friend and Marcus laughed, the sound strong and happy. "He was already meeting a friend for drinks, so we just made it here so it was easier with cars."

Relief, pure and joyous, poured through him like cold water on a hot day. He clapped his hands and rubbed them together. Though it was wrong, he really wanted Marcus all to himself tonight.

"So, what are we going to do then? Hit the clubs?" Tommy threw back the rest of his whiskey, excitement jumping in his belly. They hadn't been out dancing in so long, not since Marcus had "settled down" with his little structural engineer.

"Yeah, right, Tommy. I'm too old for that shit. Sit down and talk to me."

Tommy fell back onto the high stool with an exaggerated sigh and threw his hands up in the air like he was defeated. He actually didn't mind where they were, so long as he got to spend some time with Marcus.

"We're only thirty, Marcus, seriously? Just because you're all domesticated."

Marcus laughed and lifted his left hand, wriggling the bare fingers. "Not yet, but if I get my way, he'll marry me one day."

Tommy sobered, his heart thudding in his chest, sickening him with each slow pound. He swallowed hard.

"You're that serious?"

He knew they were, of course. The writing was all over the wall. He'd never seen Marcus so happy. And if Tommy put aside his emotions and was honest, Danny was a great guy.

"Yeah, we are."

A commotion at the bar drew their attention, and Tommy glanced up to see a handsome, enormously built guy come up to the counter and pick Danny up for a bear hug. He appeared a few years older than him and Marcus, maybe thirty-five, or a little older.

"Who the fuck is that?" Marcus' angry voice echoed Tommy's exact thoughts, though the tone was quite different from the one in his head. The guy was gorgeous. Absolutely beautiful, in a rugged, throw-you-over-his-shoulder, caveman sort of way.

Danny was soon back on the ground and grabbing the guy's hand, tugging him in their direction. Marcus jumped to his feet and Tommy smothered his laugh as he also stood. So much for being so in love he wanted to marry the guy. Didn't trust and love go hand in hand? Though, what would he know about either?

Danny practically ran up to them, bouncing like a puppy dog.

"Hey, babe, this is the friend I was telling you about, Big Bear Ben. Ben, this is my boyfriend Marcus and his best friend, Tommy."

Marcus reached out and shook the man's hand, and an inappropriate giggle burst out of Tommy's mouth. "Big Bear? That suits you so perfectly. Especially after that hug you laid on Danny."

The big bear of a man turned towards him with a wide grin as he extended his hand. As Tommy shook it, little electric currents of awareness pulsed through his palm at the first touch of skin.

Wow, this guy is hot.

"Yeah. I'm fun to take to bed for a cuddle, too."

Fuck, he's funny, too!

Tommy looked straight into the warmest brown eyes he'd ever seen.

Yummy.

"Do you guys want to sit with us?" Tommy motioned to the spare barstools around them and inwardly winced. What happened to wanting to spend the whole night Marcus alone?

Danny and Ben exchanged looks and shrugged. "Yeah, sure. Why not?"

So, they all grabbed a chair and sat down at the tall, round table. Four stools with four men, all facing one another with a drink in hand. Tommy grinned. His birthday had just gotten interesting.

Chapter Two

BEN EYED the gorgeous blond sitting next to him at the table. Tommy.

I wonder if he's as flighty as he seems.

Tommy looked dressed to impress and had obviously taken great care with his hair and skin. He practically glowed with good health and sex appeal. He might be vain, but he looked fucking delicious.

Ben leaned forward on his chair and addressed Danny's boyfriend, trying to ignore the pull on his mind to look back at Tommy. "So, Marcus, have you planned where you're traveling in Europe yet? Danny hasn't stopped talking about your trip."

Danny groaned and rolled his eyes in an exaggerated way.

"Ben, did you seriously have to bring that up?"

Marcus grinned as he threw as arm over Danny's shoulders. "Yeah, well you lost the bet, so you're coming."

Tommy leaned over the table and ruffled Marcus' hair in an affectionate yet flirty way. "If Danny won't come, I will."

A laugh bubbled up inside Ben at the outrageousness of this guy's behavior. Who would do that to another man's partner, especially in front of their boyfriend?

Danny wasn't pleased though, and hostility was rolling off him in red-hot waves.

He turned to Ben to explain, his eyes flashing with hurt and anger. "Marcus wants to show me Europe, but I don't want to go if he's going to pay for everything."

Again, Tommy laughed jovially and caressed Marcus's free shoulder. Ben could literally see Danny's annoyance in the way he shifted away from Marcus, and as he consciously had to unclench his teeth, he realized it was starting to aggravate him, too.

Marcus was Danny's boyfriend, and Tommy really had no right to be touching Marcus like that or giggling at every second thing the guy said.

Marcus swatted him away and turned his body to face Danny, but Tommy just laughed at him.

If he does it again, I'll step in to put a stop to it. For Danny's sake.

Ben had liked the kid since he had been hired to work with them a few months ago. He was kind, hard working, and completely in love with his boyfriend. He was a sweetie, and Ben didn't like seeing him upset.

Though, if he were honest, the idea of getting his hands on that lush piece of ass Tommy owned was pretty much a good incentive all on its own.

"If you can't go because of your deep seated morals, I will, Danny. I don't have money hang-ups." Tommy lifted his hand once more, and Ben's control snapped. He grabbed Tommy's barstool by the seat and pulled it towards him with a quick tug, almost throwing Tommy off in the process.

"Hey!" Tommy's blue eyes flashing as he swung around and righted himself on his seat.

Ben put his lips to Tommy's ear and growled, "If you want to grope someone so badly you can touch me, beautiful boy, but leave Danny's boyfriend alone."

Tommy gasped and shivered, the movement making Ben instinctively reach up and run a reassuring hand over the man's back. Had he just called Tommy *beautiful boy*? Oh fuck, the Dom in him had come out. It usually took months of sex with a man to get even the smallest bit of that side of him to surface. Three minutes? No way.

Tommy elbowed him gently and ignored the endearment, but he swayed closer as Ben continued to rub the man's muscled back.

"So, what was the bet?" Ben forced himself to ask, as Marcus and Danny stared at him with wide, disbelieving eyes.

"Uh ... when I was worried about my graduating marks, Marcus told me to stop stressing because I would get an average of distinction. I didn't believe him, so we made a bet. If I did do well, then I had to go to Europe with him."

Ben tried hard to concentrate on the conversation rather than the way his cock was aching. It had lengthened and was pressing agonizingly against the fly of his jeans.

"Well, you obviously scored high. Book it now for three months' time, save your salary, and go. You'll have more than enough."

Danny bit his lip and looked at Marcus. "Yeah, I suppose."

Marcus lit up like a Christmas tree, eyes sparkling, teeth flashing in a brilliant smile.

Ben slowly retracted his hand from Tommy's spine. "If you guys are in it forever, then you don't need to worry about the money shit. The way I see it, pride should never get in the way of being together. If Marcus can afford it now, let him pay. Then wait another year, and you can take him somewhere."

Ben stared at his friend and employee, trying his best not to tell him what to do but rather guide him with the knowledge he'd accumulated over time. He knew how in love Danny was with Marcus. He just needed some encouragement occasionally to not worry about the small things.

"You're right." Danny brightened visibly and planted a kiss on Marcus, then turned back to Ben. "Hang on, what about work? I haven't accrued any leave."

Ben waved his hand. "You'll have two weeks by then, and I'll talk to your boss." He winked at Danny, and he brightened even more, his blue eyes sparkling like twin sapphires.

"Thanks, Ben."

Tommy swiveled in his chair and glared at Ben, the movement weird and unexpected. "And who are you that can guarantee something like that?"

Ben smiled calmly at the aggressive stance Tommy was taking and looked back at Danny as he spoke.

"Ben's my boss. Well, he's *the* boss actually."

Ben flashed Danny a stern look. That wasn't public knowledge. "Danny."

Danny flushed pink and grinned like a kid on Christmas. "Sorry, I just think it's so cool."

Ben rolled his eyes and rocked back on his stool.

Marcus sat forward, his hand tapping on the wooden bench top. "Hang on. Ben, as in Ben Thomas? Owner of Thomas Engineering?"

Ben squirmed in his chair and looked away. He didn't really like this attention. That was why he paid people to run his company. "Well, yeah, but my passion is for the structural engineering side of things, not for the business."

And it was. He'd worked his ass off for ten years, and now he'd had enough of all the stress. He just wanted to do his job and let someone else manage his company while he did what he loved.

Tommy turned on his barstool and glared at him again, the move contorting his pretty features into something quite ugly. "You're Danny's boss and you're having Friday night drinks with him? Isn't that a bit unethical?"

Ben blinked at the blond vision next to him. "Sorry?"

Tommy clenched his jaw tight, a muscle ticking along his jaw. "Aren't there rules about sexual harassment preventing that sort of thing?"

Ben's disappointment was keen and sliced through him as effectively as a hot knife would have. He was pretty relaxed about most things, or tried to be. After so many years of stress while he built his business, he didn't need this sort of negativity in his life. A pity, considering his instant physical attraction to Tommy and the obvious need the boy had for someone to take him in hand. It had been a while since he'd felt anything like it.

Ben planted his hands on the small circular table and pushed himself to his feet. He looked straight at Danny, whose beautiful blue eyes were wide with shock.

"You want to go sit somewhere else for a bit? I can't stay long anyway."

Danny looked between them, the silence stretching around the table uncomfortable and vast. "Yeah, sure, Ben."

Ben forced his indifferent veneer over his face and turned towards the two younger men. "It was nice to meet you both."

His eyes skirted over Tommy's shocked expression and settled on Marcus. "Danny will be perfectly safe with me, I promise."

Marcus stood up and extended his hand. Ben took the gesture of friendship in his own bear-like grip, impressed with the strength of Marcus's handshake this time.

"You can have him all night just so long as he's home before dawn."

A smile rose unbidden on Ben's face. Marcus trusted him with Danny.

Good. He should.

He released Marcus' hand and turned away without looking at Tommy. Danny grabbed his arm as they walked through the bar until they found an empty table in the back.

"We can leave if you want, Ben. Go somewhere else?"

Ben shook his head and sat down in the solid leather booth. "Nah, don't be stupid. I'm too old to do anything but sit here and have a drink."

Danny scoffed loudly. "You're not too old for anything, Ben."

The annoyance Ben had tried really hard to hide boiled up, and he shot an angry glance at the wall that hid Marcus and Tommy from view. "I'm too old to put up with that sort of shit."

Danny grabbed a waitress on her way past. "Excuse me, could you bring us two Johnny Blacks with ice, please?"

"No problem." She smiled as her eyes did a cursory inspection of both of them.

Good thinking by the kid, he needed a drink. "What's his story?"

"Ignore Tommy. He's never liked me. He's nothing but a jealous asshole."

Perversely, part of Ben rose to defend Tommy. "No, I don't think so. He's just a brat who relies on his looks too much. He needs someone who won't put up with his shit to take him in hand."

Danny cocked his head in an assessing way, and Ben's cheeks filled with blood for the first time in twenty years.

Damn, I'm blushing!

The waitress arrived with their drinks and set the glasses down in front of them. Ben pulled out some money and silenced Danny's objection with a stern look. "My treat."

Danny twirled the glass in his hand. "Thanks, man. How come you don't have a partner, Ben?"

Relieved that Danny had gone down a slightly different path, Ben shrugged. "Too busy before and now I just haven't found anyone I click with."

Danny nodded with understanding and held up his tumbler of whiskey. "To good friends?"

Ben chuckled, and their glasses clinked, sloshing golden liquor around the rim. "Definitely.

Chapter Three

"YOU FUCKING IDIOT! What the hell did you do that for?"

Marcus' vehemence made Tommy jump, pulling him from his self-made stupor. He blinked at his best friend.

"What?" He cocked an arrogant eyebrow at Marcus, knowing it wouldn't work, but trying it on anyway.

"Did you seriously just question the integrity of Ben Thomas? Are you frikkin' stupid or something?"

Heat bubbled up out of nowhere, and Tommy's jaw tightened. "Yes, because I'm the stupid one, remember?"

Marcus looked affronted, but then his eyes showed understanding. "Why, Tommy? Seriously, what's up?"

That look took most of the wind out of Tommy's sails, and he slouched on his chair. "I don't know. He was just pissing me off, and I ... reacted."

"Have you been seeing anyone new?"

Tommy's head jerked back up. That was a swift change of topics.

"Sort of. A few guys, but nothing serious."

Definitely the understatement of the century. He'd had two one-night stands in the past few weeks and none for a month before that. His life sucked.

"Should we get another drink?" Marcus stood up and tilted his head toward the bar.

"Sure." Tommy pushed himself up slowly and followed his best friend to the counter. He was way too sober for it to be his birthday.

Marcus ordered them two more drinks, and Tommy skulled the whiskey before the liquid had a chance to settle in the glass.

"Another, please."

He threw the next one back just as quickly, welcoming the burn down his throat as it traveled to his gut. The warmth spread along his veins, and he leaned against the counter.

Damn, maybe I should have eaten more for dinner.

"There they are."

Tommy turned in the direction that Marcus nodded and saw Ben and Danny talking and laughing.

"You wanna go over?" Tommy asked Marcus as he swayed on his feet, heat tingling through his body.

Ben looked up at that moment and caught his eye. He appeared to do a double take, stopping mid-sentence.

Tommy's breath caught in his chest and his whole body tightened in anticipation, but for what? He didn't know, and it was scary as hell.

"Uh, I..." He didn't even attempt to finish his sentence because Ben was obviously getting ready to leave.

The man stood up then both he and Danny were walking towards them. Ben stepped around him in an obvious attempt not to touch him and that hurt, much more than it should have.

"You're going?" Tommy's voice croaked out, and he turned to face Ben, who was almost at the door.

Ben turned back, his brown eyes no longer indifferent as he nodded. "Yeah. Getting too old for late nights."

He shrugged his massive shoulders and began to turn away.

Tommy's heart began to race as he realized he might not ever see this big bear of a man again. Before he knew what he was doing, his legs had carried him to the door where Ben was hovering. His heart felt too heavy in his chest as it thudded against his ribs.

"I'll walk you out." He smiled at Ben, avoiding looking back because he knew what would be waiting for him... smug smiles and knowing looks.

"I'm pretty tough, Tommy. No one really bothers me." Ben walked through the doors and began to move down the road.

Ben's car, a black Porsche, which looked like sex on wheels with smooth lines and curves, sat waiting for him. Ben turned towards Tommy with an eyebrow raised, waiting for him to...

Fuck, what do I do now?

"I ... wanted to apologize for before. I was out of line."

Ben looked down and pushed his hands in his back pockets, flexing his shoulders so that his shirt stretched across his huge pecs. Tommy's mouth went dry. *Wow. I am so in over my head.*

"Seriously ... uh, shit." Tommy gave up and held up his hands. He couldn't do this.

Ben's huge hand snaked out and grabbed his arm, swinging him around so fast that he ended up with his back pressed up against the car and Ben firmly on him. Tommy gasped and grabbed hold of his muscled arms for balance.

Ben dropped his head and stopped, mere millimeters from Tommy's lips.

"You sure you want this? I don't want you to think I'm harassing you."

Tommy shivered as Ben's breath tingled across his skin. He shook his head forcefully. "No."

Ben didn't move, just stared down at him. "No, what? Tell me what you want, baby."

Tommy swallowed the moan that rose. This guy was one sexy bastard. That deep, husky voice was enough to make him weak at the knees. But first he had to beg a little, and rightly so considering his earlier behavior. "I want you to kiss me."

Ben didn't wait a second more. His eyes flared a little, and then he bent forward and kissed him. If you could call it that. This kiss was out of this world. Ben had thick, soft lips that demanded a response. Tommy moaned low in his throat as Ben swept his tongue inside and tasted him.

Tommy's neck muscles loosened, and his head began to tilt away from the kiss. Ben's hands moved quickly, one cupped the back of his head, anchoring him in place, while the other hand slid down to his hip.

Tommy moaned again and pushed up against the wall of muscle, needing to get closer. He ran his hands down Ben's back, stopping at the sculpted ass to squeeze hard.

Ben growled and pulled back, panting and trembling. "You are too much."

A surprised laugh flew out of Tommy. He had never been accused of being too much of anything. "You going to take me home, big man?"

Ben's cock was thick and hard between them, making Tommy's balls ache for release. He really wanted some of that.

Slowly, Ben shook his head, and Tommy's cheeks flushed with heat as his hands balled into fists.

"Let me go then, Ben."

He struggled to get up and away from this big idiot, who he'd actually thought had wanted him mere seconds ago. He pushed up against Ben's chest and glared at the bear hovering over him. Big, warm hands came down on him, pulling his arms behind his back.

Something strange surged inside Tommy as he fought and couldn't get free. A butterfly-like excitement fluttered in his belly and his heart rate increased, his pulse thumping in his ears. He cleared his throat to speak through the thickness in his tongue. "Let me go, Ben."

Ben chuckled and bit down on the cord of muscle that ran down Tommy's neck. He shuddered as another wave of longing passed over him and his shoulders unconsciously relaxed into him.

"No way, baby."

Tommy bit his lip as Ben's husky voice passed over his skin. Ben kissed along his jaw, the soft lips driving him crazy. "Well, why the hell not then? Don't you know today is my birthday?"

Oh my God, you sound like a pansy. Stop acting like a pussy.

Tommy groaned and closed his eyes. He sounded about twelve.

Ben pulled back to look at him, yet effortlessly kept Tommy immobile against the car. Ben's brown eyes were assessing and intense as they bored into him.

"Really? Well, birthday boy, I want *time* to enjoy this gorgeous body of yours, and I don't have any tonight. Go out with me tomorrow night and if you're a good boy then, I'll take you home."

Ben's voice had dropped half an octave, and if Tommy was less aroused, he would have been offended by that offer.

"Where?"

Was that his voice all breathy and needy?

Ben dropped a kiss on his lips, and Tommy pressed his pelvis harder into the man holding him so tight. A strangled, needy noise rose from Ben, and Tommy mentally high fived himself.

"Meet me here again tomorrow night and I'll take you to my favorite restaurant."

Tommy swallowed hard. He couldn't remember the last time someone had taken him out for more than a drink or even a quick fuck. Was Ben actually asking him out on a date?

"Okay. Eight o'clock?"

Ben chuckled and pressed those luscious lips to Tommy's again, licking him and withdrawing while Tommy's head spun.

"Seven. I told you, I'm too old for late nights."

Tommy looked properly at Ben, and for the first time saw the slight crow's feet at the corners of his eyes, the few grey hairs at his temples. He was older. Good. It should mean, Tommy hoped, that he had more than just casual sex on his mind.

"You're still young, Ben."

Ben slowly stepped away, pulling his keys from his pocket. "I'm too old to fuck around, Tommy. That's not what I want anymore."

He looked at Tommy as though he expected a response, and Tommy pushed himself up and off the expensive car. Did Ben really want more than that too? Well, Tommy certainly needed something to change.

"I don't know what I want, Ben, but..." His voice faltered, and he shrugged. He'd never needed more than a night or two with a hot guy, so he wasn't practiced in talking about his feelings. Now seemed like a bad time to start.

Ben pressed a button on a vehicle key and stepped forward to open his car door.

"I know, baby, but don't play around with me. I'd rather not go there if you just want a root."

Tommy reeled back, his throat aching as his struggled with the words. "No, it's not that. I just..." He stopped. What was the actual problem? Ben was being honest with him. He may as well return the favor. "I haven't had a ... relationship before."

Ben stared at him with so much intensity that heat filled Tommy's cheeks and he looked away, grateful to the night that gave him some darkness in which to hide.

When he got up the courage to look back at Ben, the big bear was just leaning against his car with his arms crossed over his huge chest and a lazy smile on his lips. "Okay. See you tomorrow at seven then?"

Tommy nodded and took another few steps back, light happiness filling his belly. Hope, a foreign emotion for him, jumped at the smallest opportunity that Ben might be able to fill the emptiness he felt inside.

Chapter Four

THE FOLLOWING NIGHT, a Saturday, Ben drove along Brunswick Street. His windows were down, and the sounds of many restaurants and eclectic music pulsed through the car. It was handy living so close to the city.

What was he going to do about Tommy? The man was gorgeous and probably smart, too. But he had a mean streak and an obvious need for a strong hand. Ben could give him that, he was sure, but did he want to?

Ben pulled up in the same place he had parked the night before and Tommy stood leaning against a light pole.

Fuck, yes. I want to tame that.

He was a walking magazine cover. Blond hair that was carefully mussed and looked like he'd just rolled out of bed. He wore a fitted leather jacket, tight jeans that outlined his lean thighs, and a pale blue shirt that was the height of metrosexual fashion. Everything about him screamed *fuck me please*. Or was Ben the only one who heard that siren call?

Pressing the button to roll down the passenger side window he called out, "Hey."

Tommy swaggered over and opened the door. "You driving?"

Ben nodded, his mouth dry from it hanging open too long. The blue shirt accentuated Tommy's amazing eyes, and Ben was having trouble breathing all of a sudden.

"Yep, hop in," he managed to say as he continued to struggle for air.

He had never been in such close proximity to such a beautiful man before, especially one he wanted so badly.

"Where are we going?" Tommy asked as he quickly did up his seatbelt and looked at Ben with eyebrows raised.

Ben glanced out the window, a little annoyed that Tommy showed no outward signs that he was happy to see him. "Just a few blocks over to a little Italian place I like."

Ben gripped the steering wheel hard and focused on the road. Why was he so flustered? He needed to relax. He took a deep breath and let his shoulders drop.

"How was your day, Tommy?"

He looked over for a second and caught the surprise in Tommy's eyes.

"Pretty good. Gym, lunch with a friend. Nothing special, really."

Ben nodded and decided to ask the obvious question. He wasn't messing about. "Are you seeing anyone at the moment?"

He pulled the car over and turned the engine off as the silence stretched, cursing himself for not asking last night.

Tommy was breathing slightly faster than he should have, and Ben turned to look at the man who he wanted to be his lover.

"Well?" he asked again.

Tommy nodded slowly, and Ben's heart sank. He thought he had been clear.

"Oh, well, then there's really no point us having dinner if you're taken."

Tommy chuckled and slid a hand over onto Ben's thigh, the pressure sending shivers down his leg. "I thought *you* were seeing me?"

Ben clenched his teeth and his palms twitched.

Oh, yeah, this boy needs a good spanking.

He leaned across the car and grabbed Tommy's shirt, tugging roughly. "Damn straight I am."

Tommy surged forward and their mouths fused together. Tommy's mouth was glorious. Soft to the touch, responsive to his kisses and addictive in taste, like cinnamon and honey.

Ben thrust his tongue slowly inside Tommy's mouth and bit Tommy's full bottom lip. His cock throbbed against his jeans, and he pulled back. He'd be a sight when they got out of the car.

"Damn." He groaned and pushed his head back into the headrest. His whole body was throbbing now. Maybe they should just skip dinner?

"I love how you kiss me," Tommy murmured and brought his fingers up to his own mouth as though to savor the imprint of Ben's lips on his.

Ben grabbed his keys. It was now or never. "Let's get inside before I decide to skip dinner altogether and simply drag you back to my place."

He got out of the car with Tommy's laughter following him. Slamming his door shut, he took a deep breath. *Cold showers, laundry, doing the dishes.* He closed his eyes and imagined the most unsexy things he could. It did the job, and his erection shrank down nicely.

"What are you doing?" Tommy's voice sounded amused, so Ben opened his eyes and smiled at the vision leaning over the car, looking at him.

"Just getting myself presentable for dinner."

Tommy chuckled again, and Ben rounded the car so they could walk side by side into the restaurant.

"Table for two, Ben Thomas," he told the cute waitress behind the desk. She gave him a once-over before indicating for them to follow her.

"You made a reservation for us?" Tommy sounded incredulous.

Ben shrugged as they sat down and picked up his menu. As if he was going to risk their date at his favorite restaurant on luck. "Yeah, they always get booked out."

It was true. The place was already half full, and it was still early. Ben glanced at the menu he knew far too well and selected pasta. "What are you going to have?" He put the menu down and watched the way Tommy chewed on his bottom lip while he read.

"Too many carbs..." Tommy muttered, and Ben almost kicked him beneath the table.

"I watched you down more than four whiskeys last night, so don't talk to me about carbs. Order something you want to eat, 'cuz I'm not sitting here watching you eat a salad."

Tommy glared at him before focusing back on the menu. A young waiter walked up, pen and notepad in hand.

"Are you ready to order?"

"Yes, I'll have the spaghetti marinara, some garlic bread, and a bottle of the..." He turned to Tommy. "Red wine okay? Or do you want to drink spirits?"

"Red's good."

Ben scanned the menu quickly and pointed to the most expensive bottle on the menu. The mark up in restaurants was ridiculous, but he wasn't drinking anything else they had on the menu.

"Very good, sir, and you, sir?" The waiter looked at Tommy.

Tommy opened his mouth, shut it again, scanning the menu then sighing heavily. "Meat-lover's pizza."

A surprised laugh burst from Ben as the waiter left them. Of all the things to order. His boy either had a good appetite or an even more wicked sense of humor.

"What?"

Ben grinned. "Meat-lover's pizza? Perfect." A hot salami joke played around in his mind, but he stopped himself from blurting it out.

Tommy tapped his fingers along the table, his eyes focused on the pristine white tablecloth. "So, you've forgiven me for last night then?"

"Of course." He wouldn't have asked Tommy out if he hadn't. He wasn't one to hold grudges.

The waiter appeared with their wine and poured them each a glass, leaving the bottle on the table.

"I understood your point, Tommy, but I'd never do anything to hurt Danny. He's a good kid."

Tommy grinned like a Cheshire cat. "*A good kid?* Just how old are you? Marcus wouldn't like that at all."

Ben took a sip of his wine and let the smooth red calm him a little. When was the last real date he'd had? *Last year? No... Yes, it probably was.* No wonder he was so nervous.

"I'll be forty next year, so yeah, to me Danny's a kid."

Tommy took a gulp of his own wine, then coughed a little. "Wow, that's nice." He picked up the bottle and had a look at the label. "I don't really drink a lot of wine, but this is good."

Ben leaned back in his chair and studied the man opposite him. Tommy's hands were graceful, his face expressive. He would be a joy to watch on a daily basis.

"Yeah, I do enjoy a nice red wine. So, my age obviously doesn't bother you?" He clenched his teeth together and mentally rolled his eyes. Why was he asking? If Tommy had a problem, he assumed the man would tell him.

"Why would it? You're successful, hot, and you've been around the block and know what you want. That sounds like a great combination to me."

Tommy gave him a sassy wink and Ben let his shoulders relax, warmth flowing over him. This was nice.

Tommy leant forward, his enthusiasm clear in his sparking blue eyes and gleaming teeth.

What are you going to ask me now?

"Tell me why you work as a normal engineer and not as the boss."

Oh, that all?

Ben smiled tightly at the waiter as their food arrived. How was he going to handle that question? Was Tommy asking because he assumed Ben couldn't handle the pressure? Or was he merely curious? He'd dealt with a lot of flack when he'd stepped down as CEO, and he still felt his hackles rise when someone asked him about it.

Tommy's pizza smelt amazing, lots of grease and bacon. Exactly what a meat-lover's pizza should smell like, and his fresh spaghetti and seafood were making his mouth water. Garlic could be added to anything and would make it better.

"Eat." He indicated to Tommy and picked up his fork.

He twirled his pasta around his fork and ate a few mouthfuls as he watched Tommy's eyes roll back in his head as he enjoyed the cheese, the meat, and the flavor of his pizza. That boy needed to eat out more often.

"So?" Tommy asked as he picked up his second slice with eager fingers.

Ben sighed, put down his fork and reached for the garlic bread. He shouldn't be avoiding the question. Tommy obviously wanted to know, and what did he have to hide?

"I worked hard for ten years to make my business successful, but I got over it. I missed just doing my job. I didn't want the stress or the massive amount of responsibility. I'm not a pencil pusher, so I just hired people to run the business. They defer to me for big decisions, and I get the best of both worlds."

Tommy nodded as he chewed and reached for his wine glass. "It sounds like you're pretty clever."

Ben drank more wine, the heavy-bodied red drenching his palate. He couldn't work out if Tommy sounded intimidated, surprised, or impressed. Either way, he was keeping his guard up for the moment.

"My dad calls me 'business savvy,' but I'm no natural genius. I had to work my ass off, but I'm glad I did."

Tommy reached for the garlic bread, and Ben inhaled some more pasta, the creaminess and garlic making him moan as he ate. Time to talk about something other than himself.

"Anyway, enough about me. What do you do, Tommy? Are you an architect like Marcus?"

Tommy nodded but frowned at the same time. "Didn't you know what I did?"

"No, why would I?"

A flash of something dark, like anger, passed over Tommy's face. "No reason. Lucky I'm pretty, I suppose, or you wouldn't have asked me out."

Whoa! Where did that come from?

Ben blinked and breathed in through his nose. He didn't want to fight, nor did he want someone who assumed he'd meant to insult him.

The instinct to bite back was on the tip of his tongue, but he swallowed it down and changed tack instead.

"You know you're pretty, Tommy, or you wouldn't put so much effort into your hair and clothes, nor the hours you spend in the gym, I'm sure." He moved his hand around to indicate Tommy's body, and the man in question looked away with an embarrassed red slash across his cheeks. "But that's not why I asked you for dinner."

Tommy looked back at him, his blue eyes more vulnerable than Ben had ever seen them. He swallowed visibly before asking, "Then why did you?"

Ben pushed himself forward. "Because I want to get to know you. Who you are, not what you do. I love the fact that you're obviously intelligent, but there's more to a man than his job."

"You think I'm intelligent?"

"Of course, I do. There's an obvious intelligence to your speech and logic, although I think you enjoy making people think you're a bit of a dumb blond."

He let the words hang in the air and Tommy stared at him for a moment, his intense blue eyes showing a layer of insecurity that Ben wanted to reassure with kisses and words.

"Yeah, well I became an architect because I like to design and draw. Not many people care that I had to study a hundred hours a week to get a good enough score in high school."

Ben lifted his wine glass. "I know the feeling. Here's to beating stereotypes and putting those ignorant idiots on their asses."

Tommy lifted his wine to his lips, his hand shaking as he took a large sip.

"So, you've had a bit of that, too?"

Ben grimaced as he swallowed his wine. "Of course, I did. I was twenty-eight when I set up my own company and looked like someone you'd hire to bounce a party, not design a skyscraper."

Tommy actually spat some of the garlic bread across the table as he choked on his laughter. "Fuck, I'm sorry."

Ben laughed and ignored it. "Why? It's true."

His shoulders unscrewed another notch, finding this strange common ground was amazingly relaxing. He'd never really thought of bonding with someone over what he considered a weakness before, but it was rather liberating.

"Are you still glad you asked?"

"Asked what?"

He was lost. Ben took another bite of his pasta.

"Are you still glad you asked me for dinner?"

"'Course." He nodded and mumbled, refusing to add anything else to that sentence. He was already being as transparent as glass, and he didn't need to add to it.

Tommy ate another piece of pizza, then pushed the half empty plate forward and leaned back, cradling the glass of wine.

"That was so good."

Ben had finished his spaghetti and eyed the leftover pizza. Was it rude to eat your date's leftovers? Bad luck if it was. "Can I have a slice?"

Tommy grinned and pushed the plate further towards Ben. "Go for it. I'm done."

Ben picked up a piece and bit into the pizza, an explosion of sausage, salt, and oily cheese flowing over his taste buds. He groaned and rolled his eyes, swallowing quickly to enjoy the feeling of fullness that came with it.

"Ben, I know that you aren't what you do, but I think it's amazing that you own your own company."

Ben shrugged and finished his wine. Eyeing the half full bottle, he left his glass empty. He'd had enough already and if he drank any more, he wouldn't be able to drive.

"Yeah, it's gratifying. But it's not everything."

He was proud of what he had achieved, but he wanted more than money. It was damn lonely.

"Really, most people consider what you've achieved to be the pinnacle of life."

Ben snorted. "Yeah? Who? I'd like to see what they've got that they think work is everything."

Tommy was staring at him again.

"What?"

"What else is there to life that you want, Ben?" Tommy's words, softly spoken whilst he peered through his eyelashes at Ben, were enough to make him almost come on the spot.

Fuck, how he wanted this guy.

"Come home with me and I'll show you." The words were out of his mouth before he'd consciously decided to say them, and now that he had, it was perfect.

Tommy's smile lit up his whole face as he set his wine down. "Good. Let's go."

Butterflies took flight inside Ben's stomach as he stood up and followed Tommy to the counter. It had been so long since he'd taken anyone home to his apartment.

Tommy took out his wallet, but Ben just motioned to the man wearing the white hat. "Just pop it on my account, Tony."

The owner waved from the kitchen, and Tommy glared at him. "That's not fair."

Oh, everything's fair in love and war, baby.

Ben grabbed Tommy's hand and pulled the stubborn, gorgeous boy out of the restaurant and towards his car.

"Next time, you can pay."

He patted his date on his tight butt, hopped into his Porsche, put the car into gear and slammed his foot on the accelerator. Thank God he lived so close.

Chapter Five

THEY STEPPED into Ben's penthouse apartment, and Tommy glanced around. It was perfect. Clean. White. Modern.

He took off his leather jacket and deliberately threw it across the room. It landed on the perfect blue rug, which lay over perfect white carpet.

"I think you need a little disorder in your life, Ben."

Ben grabbed him and turned him around. Hot lips pressed down on his as he was maneuvered backwards in a whirlwind. Tommy returned Ben's kiss but didn't put up a token of resistance as he was manhandled across the room. He needed everything he was being given and sighed as his eyelids slid closed. His spine hit a plaster wall and another wall of warm, heavy muscle pressed up against his front.

Ben broke away, breathing hard. "Baby, you're going to need a safe word."

Tommy blinked, fear creeping into his belly, cold and intense. "Wh-at?"

Tommy could hear the trepidation in his own voice and cleared his throat before asking his next question. He'd seen some strange shit over the last ten years, including lots of bondage and domination stuff. He'd never been into any of it, though it looked sexy as fuck. To be controlled like that ... he shivered just thinking about it. "Are you a fucking Dom or something?"

Ben smiled one of those sexy, confident smiles and very slowly stretched Tommy's arms high above his head. He didn't resist, even when his muscles stretched tight. "I'm not in the lifestyle or anything, but I do like it a bit rough. Not many men inspire me, but you..."

Tommy shivered and arched his back to get closer. He needed to know. He wanted to be special. Just once.

"Me ... what?"

Ben growled and swooped in for a hard kiss. His lips were demanding, hot, and Tommy's eyes closed to better absorb the feel of them against him. Demanding his submission, sharing his passion.

When Ben raised his head, his eyes were dark with lust. "You make me want to spank you 'til I can see my handprints on your flesh, then fuck you so long and hard you'll still feel me next week."

Tommy moaned and lifted a leg to wrap around Ben's muscled waist. Ben put one huge hand under his ass and lifted, supporting him while Tommy wrapped both legs around him. He wanted that. He *needed* that. To have someone crave him to the point of wanting to possess him was an exciting thing.

"I want that, please."

His cock was leaking. He could feel pre-cum dampen his underwear, his balls tight and drawn up near his body.

The big bear bit down on Tommy's lower lip, and he gasped at the acute stab of pain. "Choose a word. One you would never normally use in bed."

Tommy pulled down with his arms but found he couldn't. Bear had his wrists held secure within one of his own. He wasn't going anywhere, and the powerlessness was damn exciting.

"Aahhh." He searched his mind and drew a blank. Bear ground his hard cock into Tommy's thigh, and he moaned as heat slid over his spine. "Banana."

A slow, soft chuckle emerged from Ben as he lifted his head and looked down on Tommy. "Banana, it is."

Ben released his arms and put both hands on Tommy's ass. He squeaked a little as he was lifted effortlessly away from the wall and carried into Ben's bedroom.

Tommy held on tightly as Ben fell forwards, landing with a bounce on the soft mattress, Ben's heavy form above him.

"Oof." All the air whooshed out of his lungs, and Ben pushed up with his arms, the weight on his chest lifting.

"Sorry, baby."

Desperate not to destroy the mood, Tommy shook his head and reached up for his man, pulling Ben's head back down for another kiss. He needed to feel his skin and pulled at Ben's shirt, the buttons getting in the way.

The larger man stopped Tommy's groping with his hands. "Hang on."

He stood up and slipped the shirt from his body, his massive chest finally revealed. Tommy sat up to watch the show.

"Wow." Tommy's eyes drank in every inch of heavy muscle. "How much do you work out?"

Ben shrugged and unzipped his pants. "I do power lifting. It's about strength rather than muscle definition. The saying is: more go than show."

Tommy laughed. He liked the sound of that, and it suited Ben down to a tee. He was useful, no flashy show pony. Tommy's throat constricted awkwardly as he swallowed hard, watching Ben push his pants and underwear down his legs.

Ben's heavy, hard cock sprang forth, its red head huge and rounded.

I need to taste that.

Tommy slipped down to the floor on his knees and took the mushroom-shaped head into his mouth. His skin was hot, and the scent of Ben's groin was pure male. Sweat, salt, and sex.

"Oh, fuck..." Ben's curse was pure music to his ears as Tommy slipped the shaft further into his mouth. Ben tasted of salty, warm skin. Baby soft silk over steel. The perfect combination.

Tommy reached up and cupped Ben's heavy balls, weighing them and enjoying the way Ben sighed as he slid a possessive hand around the base of his skull. He began to move, taking as much as he could into his mouth and using his tongue to trace the lip on the head.

Ben tugged on his hair and dragged him back away, pin prickles of pain making him move off the most delicious tasting cock he had ever enjoyed. His hair was pulled down, and he was forced to look up, Ben reaching down to trace his lips with his fingers.

"Get naked, baby."

Tommy grinned and jumped to his feet. He grabbed for his tight shirt and then slowed his movements, loving the heat in the air, the anticipation unfurling in his belly. He pushed his jeans down and shimmied out of them as gracefully as possible. Then he stood up and gave his date a cocky smile, his fingers tapping at his sides.

Ben's brown eyes slid over him, lingering on Tommy's cock and circling him slowly. Tommy shivered, loving the suspense, yet anxious to get started. Ben was a top, he'd have to be. Well, he'd better be, because Tommy craved to feel Ben inside him.

"You're beautiful, baby."

Tommy laughed, glad Ben thought so. "Obviously not that beautiful, or you wouldn't be just looking."

Smack. The loud sound of his ass being spanked made him jump higher than the pain of physical impact, though his butt was stinging now.

"Ow! What was that for?"

Ben spanked him again, softer this time. "You were being impatient. Now go lie on the bed on your back. I need something to tie you up with."

Tommy's knees almost buckled, and he stumbled to the bed. Ben was going to do what?

He crawled up onto the mattress and flipped over, his cock rock-hard and leaking onto his stomach. The sheet scraped against his now sensitive ass, and he shifted slightly. "You're obviously not put off by the idea," he muttered to his cock.

Ben came back into the bedroom from what Tommy assumed was a walk-in wardrobe, holding several silk ties.

"And what are you going to do with those?" Tommy cocked an eyebrow at his soon-to-be-lover as his heart did a little misstep in his chest. Sex for him in the past had been a way to get off. Quick, relatively satisfactory, and impersonal. He had the feeling that being with Ben was not going to be any of those things.

"I'm going to tie your arms and legs together and have my way with you."

Tommy groaned and held out his arms. He liked the sound of that. Kinky and sexy. "Well, hurry then."

Ben reached forward and pinched his nipple, hard. Tommy yelped and pulled back again with a glare. "What was that for?"

Ben knelt on the bed, his cock bobbing in front of him. "You're being a brat. I'm in charge, remember? Hands."

Tommy held them out reluctantly, looking off to the side. This wasn't really what he signed up for, being ordered around like a child. How was that sexy? Ben pulled Tommy's legs together and wrapped one of the ties around his ankles in a figure eight fashion. It was tight but not uncomfortable. Then he bent forward and slipped his lips around the head of Tommy's cock and sucked, hard.

"Fuck!" Tommy arched his hips and thrust up, pushing his cock down Ben's throat. Wet warmth enveloped him, making his heart race and his body tingle.

Ben moved on him, up and down until he screamed from the tingles running down his legs. His balls tightened, and his cock screamed that he was ready to come. He gripped Ben's head, only to have his lover come off him with a pop. He gasped as the feelings drained away. "Don't stop. I was almost there."

Ben chuckled and held out the second tie. "Give me your hands."

Tommy thrust his wrists at Ben, eager to do anything his lover wanted just so that he could come as soon as possible. Toughened silk wrapped around his wrists, and Tommy wiggled, the vulnerability of the position becoming clear as he lost the ability to use his hands. Ben could do anything he wanted to him now.

Ben swung a huge thigh over Tommy's body and settled on his abdomen, the warmth and weight another way of restraining him. "Now I can enjoy you."

He leaned forward, and Tommy stretched up to meet him, Ben's warm lips gentle and in no hurry as they met his.

Calm down and enjoy it!

Tommy forced his tight muscles to relax as he cupped Ben's chin with his bound hands. Ben shuddered a little and moved down, kissing and licking Tommy's skin as he went. His teeth found Tommy's nipple, and he gasped at the pleasure that was sharpened by the pain.

Ben moved down further so that he was half lying on Tommy. Ben's hot flesh burned against his skin, making Tommy want to keep him there forever. A comfort washed over him as the need to pull him even closer rose like a surging wave.

Tommy closed his eyes and focused on Ben's lips and teeth marking his belly. Suction on his lower abs made him look down to watch as Ben gave him a hickey.

He watched until it begun to sting, and he gasped. Ben came off and looked up. His eyes were lust-filled and hard, as though he were challenging Tommy to stop him.

No way. Do whatever you like.

"Marking me?" Tommy asked, his voice cracking on the question.

Ben nodded and moved further down, kissing the top of Tommy's cock and making his balls ache.

He pulled at the tie around Tommy's ankles but left the one tying his wrists so he could move, but still feel the restriction around his hands.

"Roll over, baby, and up on your knees. Take your time, though. You don't want to hurt yourself"

* * *

Tommy struggled for a minute with his hands trussed, but he rolled over and pushed up, so his gorgeous body was finally open for him.

Tommy wiggled his hips and ass, and Ben grinned to himself. His boy was in a hurry, but he'd learn soon enough that there was no need to rush. They had all the time in the world, and at his age, he'd earned some pretty good control.

That gorgeous, tight ass came up as Tommy got onto his knees, his ankles still together.

"Good boy." Ben knelt behind Tommy, his cock leaking, begging him to end both of their torments. No fucking way. He wasn't even halfway done.

"Use lots of lube." Tommy wiggled his ass in the air, and Ben spanked him just for fun. His hand stung a little, and a red mark rose on Tommy's gorgeous backside.

Yeah, I'm loving that.

"Hey! You've gotta stop doing that!"

Ben noticed that Tommy didn't move away though. In fact, he wiggled a little closer.

"You know your safe word. Use it and I stop, but I want to make this ass nice and red before I fuck you."

Tommy held very still for a minute, then nodded his head ever so slightly. Triumph filled Ben and he began to rain slaps down on to Tommy's beautiful ass and the backs of his thighs. His body was tight and young, his skin taut and smooth. He was an absolute pleasure to touch. "I want to mark you as mine, make you remember me tomorrow."

Tommy groaned and pushed back wantonly. "Don't think ... that will be ... a problem."

Ben smacked Tommy hard once more, and his lover squeaked. He couldn't stop himself as he massaged the globes of Tommy's ass with both hands, held it open and leaned forward to taste him.

"Ahh. Yes!" Tommy's shout of satisfaction spurred Ben on as he rained kisses down onto the hot skin of Tommy's ass, licking and kissing the pink flesh and diving back between the cheeks to his little puckered hole. Dipping his tongue in, he fucked Tommy's ass, stretching and lubricating the tight flesh.

"Oh please, Ben ... please."

Ben reached for the condom and lube he had placed within reach and sheathed himself. He squeezed the base of his cock for a moment, stifling his groan. Fuck, he was hard.

He popped the top on the bottle of lube and smeared his hands with it.

"You're doing so well, baby." He pushed two fingers into Tommy, who groaned and pushed back. He scissored inside and stretched the tissue, taking his time. Then he pushed two digits deep inside, searching and fingering Tommy's prostate until he was crying out to him.

Ben needed something more. A total obliteration of Tommy's senses.

"Turn over again."

Tommy groaned and rolled slowly, half out of it, his eyes dazed as if he were on drugs. "You're going to kill me."

Ben chuckled and picked up the third tie. Once Tommy was

settled onto his back, Ben lifted his legs and arms up, tying them together so he was hog tied.

"What the hell?"

Ben pushed Tommy's legs back towards his head so that his ass came up, knelt over him and lined up his cock. "Oh, yeah."

He pushed the head into Tommy and thrust deep, until his balls slapped Tommy's flesh and the most amazing warmth wrapped around him.

"Ah!" Tommy arched his back and clamped tightly around Ben's cock. He froze, eyes squeezed shut as his body screamed in delight. Pleasure hit him in the gut, and heat washed over his spine.

Ben forced his eyes open again and looked down, seeing Tommy's face around his bound legs.

"You okay, baby?"

Tommy looked up, his eyes frantic. "Fuck me, please."

A quiver of a smile reached Ben's mouth, and he began to move. He liked that, the begging. He'd like a little more of it next time.

In and out he thrust, keeping the pace slow, while Tommy fought him all the way. He tugged on his bound hands and kicked with his legs. "Move faster! I need more."

Ben sped up his strokes, pulling back so that he would hit Tommy's prostate right on.

"Ah! Yes! There!"

Ben pistoned in and out, his hot flesh slapping against Tommy's body. Sweat rolled down his back as he flexed his hips over and over, Tommy's needy cries impossible to ignore. "There, baby? Is that the spot?"

"Fuck! I'm going to come, please, fuck ... please."

Ben wasn't stroking Tommy's cock, and he wanted to see if Tommy would come from this alone. He clenched his teeth hard and held onto his control, though his balls were aching for release and the temptation of all the pleasure that awaited him, calling like a siren.

He dug his fingers into Tommy's thighs and pulled him up hard as he fucked him. Tommy's screams filled the air as he came, his ass clenching down on Ben in an unforgiving way.

Ben let go, pumping his seed into the condom, filling Tommy's ass. His eyes slid shut as his whole being rippled with pleasure, a deep groan rolling out of him as heat flooded his body.

He sagged back down, resting onto his haunches and slowly pulling out of the tight clasp of Tommy's ass.

Ben shook his head to clear the fog and quickly untied Tommy's arms and legs that were now shaking with the strain.

Tommy collapsed back against the mattress, sexy white lines of cum decorating his chest. His eyes were closed, his cheeks flushed. He looked exhausted and so perfect lying in Ben's bed that a flutter of something strange happened in Ben's chest.

Ben forced himself to climb away. He threw the condom in the bin and cleaned himself up. Then he wet a washcloth with warm water and headed back to the room.

Tommy hadn't moved. In fact, he looked asleep.

Softly moving the face washer over Tommy's chest, he cleaned him up and threw it back into the bathroom. Should he lie down again? He didn't want to wake him up.

Tommy's blue eyes flickered open. "Whatcha doing?"

Ben climbed onto the bed and pulled the blankets back. "I didn't want to wake you."

Tommy groaned as he pulled himself to a sitting position. "Do you want me to go home?"

Ben growled at him, angry and a little hurt that his lover would think he would want such a thing. "Are you kidding me? Lay your ass back down."

Tommy rolled under the covers, his excited smile lighting Ben up from the inside out. So, he hadn't wanted to leave. *Good.*

Ben lay on his back and reached out for his lover, pulling Tommy onto his chest and curling a possessive arm around him.

"How long's it been since you came with nothing on your cock?"

Tommy nuzzled into the curve of Ben's shoulder and sighed. "Never have before."

A maniacal grin rose as satisfaction settled over him. He frowned, trying to sound serious as he spoke, "Good. Now go to sleep. I'm going to hold you all night."

Tommy sighed again and snuggled closer. Peace settled over Ben like a warm blanket as he fell straight down into sleep.

Chapter Six

HE WAS WARM, too warm. Tommy forced his eyes open as he registered several things at once. One, he was naked. Since when did he sleep naked? And two... Ben's huge bulk was nestled up behind him.

Heat. Comfort. Peace.

All those feelings buffeted Tommy, and he settled deeper into Ben's embrace. What a wild night. The big bear had dominated him from the start, and he had experienced the most mind-blowing sex of his life. It had been awesome.

He'd never had a guy really take control like that before. True, he usually bottomed, but this had been completely different. Ben had made sure that Tommy's pleasure was first and foremost, but at the same time took his own pleasure at his own pace. It had been exactly what Tommy needed, and he wanted more.

"Good morning," Ben grumbled in his ear as he kissed Tommy's neck and rolled quickly out of bed.

Tommy moved over to his back and turned his head to watch Ben's gorgeous ass and massive frame disappear into what he assumed was the bathroom.

Sounds of Ben relieving himself made Tommy smile as he stretched his arms above his head and wiggled his sore ass against the sheets. That spanking had been fucking hot, but he was bruised now.

When Ben returned, his morning hard-on still half there, Tommy rushed to the toilet and relieved himself, too. He needed more of his big teddy bear. Standing in the doorway, arms either side of the frame, he wiggled his hips a little.

"Up for an encore this morning?"

Ben, who was sitting on the bed, lay back against the pillows and began stroking his own cock. "Hmm, maybe..."

Tommy watched Ben's cock get harder and thicker. Then Ben began to moan, and Tommy swallowed hard at the lust he saw in Ben's eyes. He stared deep into those dark brown eyes, unable to look away.

Putting his own hand on his cock, he stroked it in time with his lover. Ben watched him with hungry eyes, and his spine began to stiffen. "Come over here and come on me."

Tommy grinned as his balls began to ache. He had never heard anything so dirty, and he couldn't wait to do it. Staggering forward, he gasped as his cock throbbed with pleasure.

"You are so fucking hot, baby," Ben croaked, changing his grip and moving his hand faster.

Tommy didn't want to stand there apart from Ben any longer and moved down so that he was lying beside him, a hand under his head so that he could watch Ben's face.

Ben wrapped an arm around his back whilst Tommy laid his leg over Ben's. He loved this, the connection. Hot and a little sweaty, he arched and groaned. They moved together, gyrating against each other as they chased their orgasms.

"Gonna ... soon..." Ben grunted and leant forward for a kiss. Tommy opened his lips and sucked on Ben's tongue, earning a growl from the bigger man.

Tommy pulled back from the steamy kiss and stroked his own

cock, watching as Ben's eyes opened wide and stared straight at him as he came. Hot seed covered his belly and chest as Ben groaned and shook next to him.

Tommy came without meaning to, his orgasm surprising him as it tore through him while he watched his lover. "Oh, fuck..."

He blasted all over Ben's thigh and belly, their cum mingling to create the hottest image Tommy had ever seen. Shockwaves passed through him, and he closed his eyes on a moan. *So fucking good!*

Ben grabbed the back of Tommy's head and pulled him in for a hot, possessive kiss, before they both pulled away panting.

"That was so good," Ben groaned and stretched, looking down at his chest. "I need a shower."

Tommy laughed and rolled out of bed again, his legs weak and shaking. "Let's go, then."

He staggered to the bathroom, chuckling to himself. Being with Ben was like being on a drug. He was high as a kite.

Ben stepped up behind him, his sticky torso pressing against Tommy's spine. Tommy leaned back, unable to resist the compulsion to be close to him.

"In you go, baby. My shower's big enough for two."

Tommy stumbled forward into the shower, turning the water on and stepping out the way of the cold blast.

"What are you up to today?" Ben asked him as he adjusted the temperature to suit them.

Tommy shrugged, a strange, panic-like sensation settling into his gut. "Nothing much. A bit of shopping and stuff."

He had to do some laundry and cleaning actually. Tommy's apartment looked like a clothing bomb had exploded. *Organized chaos* he called it, though it was getting less and less organized.

"Yeah, I get that. You live alone too?"

Tommy nodded slowly. Strange how you could feel so close to someone yet know just about nothing about them.

"Yep. I grew up in Camberwell, and my parents still live there.

But I bought a two-bedroom apartment at the Docklands as soon as I could afford to move out."

Ben chuckled and moved under the spray of water as Tommy reached for the soap.

"I remember that feeling oh so well."

Ben scrubbed himself down, rinsing off the evidence of their night together. He really was spectacular to look at. His muscle bulk was huge. Tommy felt skinny in comparison, and he worked hard to stay as muscled as he was.

Ben looked down at him. "You wanna get together during the week?"

Tommy's belly fluttered, and he ran the soap over his own body. He wanted to see Ben again, too much. "Yeah, maybe next weekend?"

Ben's smile fell, and he turned away to wash his face under the water. An uncomfortable knot formed in Tommy's gut, but he couldn't take it back. Everything was happening too fast.

"My work's pretty full on, Ben. I crash most nights during the week."

Ben stepped out of the spray and took the soap from Tommy. "Yeah, no problem." His tone was light, but he wouldn't look at Tommy anymore.

Tommy sighed and stepped under the hot water. *I'm so fucking confused! What do I do now?* Being with Ben was awesome, but he felt like he was drowning in totally foreign waters.

He stepped out of the shower and reached for a towel, water clinging to his hot skin. Drying himself quickly, he wrapped the towel around his waist, anxious to get moving now. He needed some space. "Marcus and Danny are having a party next Saturday night. Are you going?"

Ben turned and looked at him for the first time in what seemed like hours, though in truth it was only a few minutes. The he shook his head. "Danny hasn't said anything to me."

Tommy ran a hand through his wet hair and pushed forward despite his instincts that screamed to run. Run far away from this amazing man who was just too much for someone like him. How was he going to keep this man happy in the long run?

"Come. I'm sure Danny and Marcus would like you there."

Ben turned the water off and stepped out of the shower, his huge cock swinging between his thighs. Tommy stifled the moan that rose once again and moved into the bedroom for his clothes. He ached with how much he wanted this man.

Dropping the towel, he picked up his jeans, stepping into them and covering himself as quickly as possible. He heard a chuckle behind him.

"You know your ass has my handprint on it?"

Tommy grabbed his shirt and slipped it on, feeling the heat in his cheeks return. He knew he had Ben's mark on him. "Yep, here too." He turned and pointed at the hickey Ben had made on his stomach before covering it up with his shirt.

Ben nodded, his eyes serious. "So you won't forget me too quickly."

Tommy sighed heavily, not sure how to handle this. He needed to be honest with Ben, but how could he be when he wasn't even sure how he felt? He sat down in the beautiful armchair and pulled on his shoes. "Ben, last night was awesome, but I just don't know how to do this."

He looked up and stared at his lover, hoping to God Ben would take control again and help him.

Ben moved forward and squatted down in front of Tommy. "Okay, look. We'll go slow. Do you want me to pick you up and we can go to Marcus' party together?"

Tommy chewed on his lip. That was asking a bit much, wasn't it? Then he'd have to rely on Ben to get home. "Can I meet you there? I kinda like having my own car."

Ben dropped his head and inhaled sharply through his nose.

Tommy began to get annoyed. He was a thirty-one-year-old man for goodness' sakes! He stood up and moved away from the big bear still squatting on the floor. "Well, it's true. I don't have my car now, so you have to either take me home or I call a taxi. It's just inconvenient, Ben."

Ben stood up and grabbed Tommy's towel off the floor, stalking into the bathroom and placing them both back neatly on the rack. *Neat freak!*

Naked now, he moved back into the room and strode into the walk-in wardrobe.

Tommy couldn't stop from staring at him. All that lithe, natural grace in such a big man. He was awesome to watch. *Not bad to kiss, lick, and touch, either.* He was still staring at the empty doorway when Ben re-emerged, now dressed in casual trousers and a tight, white t-shirt.

"I'll drop you home then and we can meet up next Saturday."

Tommy's chest squeezed tight, and actual tears burned at the back of his eyes. He cleared his throat roughly and grabbed his keys from the floor where they had dropped.

"Thanks. That'd be good."

They drove in silence, and Ben didn't even kiss him goodbye. What was more shocking was the pain it caused deep in Tommy's chest. As he stepped out of the car, his heart jumped when Ben called out to him.

"Tommy. Here's my card with all my numbers on it. Do you have one I can have?"

Tommy fumbled with his wallet, pulling out a business card that had most of his details on it. He handed it through the window and took Ben's with his other hand.

"My card doesn't have my mobile on it."

Ben nodded stiffly, his mouth pulling down on one side. "Well, mine does, so if you want to message me you can."

Tommy pulled back, the weight of those words settling onto his shoulders.

"See ya next weekend then," Ben called as he waved and drove away.

Tommy stood on the pavement and lifted his hand in silent farewell as he watched the Porsche drive away.

The week went so damn slowly for Ben. Every single minute until Saturday dragged by. Each morning he woke and reached for his mobile, but there was never anything there from Tommy.

He worked every day and avoided Danny's questions about what had happened with Tommy on Friday night. Fortunately, the kid had now invited him to their party, so he felt better about going.

But what to do about the little brat who had graced his bed on Saturday night?

Ben had never had sex like that before, ever. He had fantasized about it, wanted it. But he'd never had the guts to actually act on his dominant desires, and he'd never found a man who had made him want it so much.

With Tommy, it was as easy as breathing. The other man needed it, and that made Ben want to give it to him.

Even crazier, Ben knew he was in serious danger of falling in love with the gorgeous blond. Tommy was intelligent, beautiful, cheeky, and far too lovable. Those blue eyes that screamed "fuck me" also pulled up every protective instinct he had.

Tommy needed to be loved, to feel wanted and protected. Ben was sure he could do that if the man would let him close enough.

Saturday night was going to be interesting, indeed.

Chapter Seven

BEN KNOCKED on the door of Marcus and Danny's apartment, placing the bottles of alcohol down before he dropped them, and stuffed his hands into his jean pockets.

"Fuck." He didn't know how he was feeling, but terrified was a good word for the trembling in his hands.

The door swung open, and Danny stood there, looking beautiful in an orange t-shirt and cargo pants.

"Ben!"

Ben stepped forward and grabbed him up in a hug, grateful that at least one person was happy to see him. He had no fucking idea how Tommy was going to respond. The little shit hadn't texted or called all week.

Someone clapped him on the back, and he put Danny down to turn to Marcus, who was smiling at him also. "Good to see you, Ben. Glad you could make it."

Ben stepped back into the doorway to collect the bottles of good whiskey and red wine he'd brought with him. "Wasn't sure what you guys drank, but these are nice."

Marcus took the bottles and whistled. "Very nice. Thanks heaps. Come in."

They closed the door, and Ben was led through the apartment into the kitchen. The place was nice. Clean, bright, great light and huge, open plan spaces.

There were already about twenty people there, mostly guys, but Ben couldn't see Tommy anywhere.

"Drink, Ben?"

Hell, yes!

"Yeah. Beer, if you've got it."

Marcus moved to the fridge, pulled out a beer and popped the top, handing it to Ben with the flourish of a confident man. Ben smiled as he watched Marcus pull Danny into his side, possessive and strong.

"This is some place, Marcus."

Marcus took a swig of his own beer then placed it down on the marble top bench.

"Wanna tour?"

Ben nodded, fear tightening his gut. Where was Tommy holed up?

"Kitchen, dining, lounge." Marcus waved at the large, comfortable space, and Ben nodded his head politely. He followed behind Marcus while Danny wandered off to talk to some other guests.

"This is the spare room..." Marcus flung open the door, and there was Tommy. Leaning up against the wall, his head thrown back in a laugh. He was with another man.

Ben's stomach lurched and dropped so suddenly it was like someone had come up and punched him in the gut. His eyes were still taking in the scene before him because he seriously couldn't believe this was happening. He watched for another second, and then Tommy turned and spotted him. Those blue eyes went wide with shock, and Ben inhaled sharply as his ribs squeezed tight before he turned and strode away.

His heart was beating so hard he was beginning to feel sick as he staggered back to the lounge and sank down onto the couch. Tommy's face, alight and happy—he'd been alone with that young guy. They hadn't been touching, but the atmosphere had been heavy with promise.

"Fuck." His hands were trembling again, and he clenched them into tight fists.

"Hey, man, you okay?" Marcus dropped onto a chair close by and looked over, his eyebrows drawn together with worry.

Ben nodded, his nerves frayed, his shoulders tight. He felt like he'd gone ten rounds with a boxer, and all he'd done was see Tommy with another guy for two seconds.

"You and Tommy?" Marcus asked quietly, and Ben looked up, nodding slowly. How else was he going to explain his reaction?

"They were just talking." Marcus smiled, shrugging.

"Yeah, in a room with a bed and a closed door." Ben couldn't help the bitterness lacing his words. He was just so goddamn disappointed! And if he were honest, his heart ached a little more than it should, too.

At that moment, Tommy came into the room. He looked around, his eyes finding Ben. Red slashed across his high cheekbones, and he smiled hesitantly.

Ben looked his fill of the man who had haunted his dreams all week. He was even more beautiful than Ben remembered, if that was possible.

Tommy walked forward, his gait loose and confident.

"Hey, Ben."

Ben nodded and sat up a little straighter, his Dom tendencies coming to the front. Hadn't he left enough of a mark on this guy to make him remember who he belonged to?

"Hey, yourself."

Tommy's smile faltered for a minute and they locked gazes, tension sizzling between them like a naked wire.

"Ah … hey, Phil." Marcus coughed lightly.

The guy Tommy had been holed up with walked up and gave them a charming smile. "Hey."

Tommy turned to do the introductions. "Ben, this is Phil, a university friend of Marcus' and mine. Phil, this is Ben, Danny's boss."

Phil's face lit enthusiastically and held out his hand. "Oh, hey! It's great to finally meet you. Danny talks about you all the time."

Ben shook the good-looking man's hand reluctantly, though realizing quickly that the guy was gay and probably a good fellow didn't take away the sting.

"Thanks. Always nice to meet any friend of Tommy's."

Phil laughed and bumped his hip into Tommy's. "We go way back." He laughed to himself, and Ben clenched his fists tight on his thighs, pushing himself to his feet.

"Where's your bathroom, Marcus?"

Marcus pointed towards the hallway. "There's a couple, but you can use my en-suite if you want. Bedroom is second door on the left."

Ben forced himself to look back at Phil. "Nice to meet you. Excuse me."

Vibrating with anger, he moved stiffly through the apartment, ignoring the interested stares of the men around him. He opened the door to Marcus' bedroom, absently noting the beautiful linen, the expensive furniture, and moved to the bathroom. Again, it was amazing. The fittings, the tiling, everything was immaculate.

Ben put his hands down on the basin and hung his head. He had to get out of here. He had been stupid to think that Tommy wanted anything more than a quick fuck, and he had been the idiot who had handed over more than he should have.

"Ben?" The familiar voice caressed him, and he shivered in acknowledgment.

Tommy. Fuck. Just go away.

He ran the water and splashed some on to his face, patting his cheeks dry with one of the soft hand towels.

"Yeah?" He placed the white towel back exactly how he had found it and stepped into the bedroom.

He quirked an eyebrow at Tommy and crossed his arms over his chest. They were going to have this out once and for all, it seemed.

"It wasn't what it looked like."

Ben smirked and dropped his arms down to his sides. That was the best he could do?

"Really? Well, it looked like you were about to lock the door and fuck the guy."

He glared at his lover, watching the way Tommy's eyes widened and he shook his head slowly. "No, we were just talking."

"Yeah, right, Tommy. You knew I was coming tonight to see you, so if you were trying to let me know you aren't available, message received loud and clear. Although you could have just told me. I made it perfectly clear to you last weekend that I didn't want to play games."

Ben saw the way Tommy's face paled as he'd spoke and knew he'd hit the nail on the head. Fuck! He'd hoped like hell he'd been wrong this time.

Tommy forced himself to swallow, the movement awkward and obvious. He hadn't meant to give Ben that impression at all.

"No, it's not that."

Ben rolled his eyes and moved around him as though he were going to leave.

Tommy panicked and moved back against the door, his spine making a thump as he pressed against it. "No, stay!"

Ben wheeled back, hands clenched at his sides. "Move out of the way, Tommy."

Tommy shook his head and stalked forward. "No, it wasn't like that! I used the toilet. Then he came in, and we just started talking."

Ben laughed bitterly and made to walk out again, but Tommy put his hands out and grabbed Ben's huge pecs, the muscles flinching under his hands.

"Ben, honestly. Please, don't go."

Ben moved back into the room, but his eyes were hard. "Look, it's fine. I should have known you wanted nothing more than a fuck when you suggested to meet me here. I should've known better."

Heat began to simmer in Tommy's blood. Now he was a flighty little slut?

"Why? Because I just talked to some other guy and wanted to bring my own car? That's not fucking fair, and you know it!"

Tommy moved away from the door, joining Ben in the room. If the man wanted to leave, he could go right ahead and walk out.

"Oh, I get it. You fucked me and it was fun, but you can't be bothered talking to me and asking me how I actually feel. I might be blond, but I'm not fucking stupid, Ben!"

Before Tommy could decide whether he was staying or going, Ben stepped close and gripped his short blond hair, tugging and pulling his face up for a punishing kiss before dragging his lips down the side of Tommy's neck. Tommy moaned at the sheer heat and desire embedded within the movements. He could do nothing but gasp against the pleasure tinged with pain as he clung to his lover.

"Don't think this color fools me, Tommy." Ben tugged Tommy's blond hair again and moved to lick Tommy's collarbone. "You may choose to be blond, my boy, but you're smart and beautiful and funny. I may be wrong about that, but I don't think I am. But since you have gone to all the trouble to make me feel like shit, I think you better start proving I can trust you. Admit what you did tonight was wrong and thoughtless, or I'm walking out of here forever."

Tommy offered Ben his throat and swallowed hard as hot tears filled his eyes.

"No, I want the words, Tommy!"

"I…" He'd never been able to express how he felt about anyone, but as he concentrated on Ben's tight grip on his body, he let the words go. "I'm sss-sorry, Ben. I didn't think about how you felt. About any of it. I was just trying to be independent."

"That's a fucking bad excuse."

Tommy gulped. "I'm not used to trusting anyone or being close to anyone. I don't know how to act."

"Well, how about you ask me?"

Tommy nodded and whispered this time, "What should I have done, Ben?"

"You should have come with me, held my hand, sat on my lap, and let me adore you. And you most certainly should not have gone off to the bathroom with some guy. If you don't want me, you just say the words, Tommy."

He grabbed hold of Ben's arm. "No, I do. I'm sorry. I didn't think. I'm just… I didn't mean to hurt you, and I won't do it again."

His throat ached from trying to talk through the tears, but it was getting easier. He didn't want to lose this guy by being an idiot, and he had been.

"I'm sorry, Ben."

"Good boy. I see what you show everyone else, but it's not you. I see the *real* you. The one you try to hide away."

Tommy gasped as Ben's hands turned him around. He swallowed with difficulty before asking, "Yeah, so what do you see?"

The big bear lifted his head and stared into Tommy's eyes. "I see a boy who forgot that he's mine."

Oh, thank you. I haven't lost him yet.

Those stupid tears threatened again, so Tommy tilted his head back, exposing more of his neck to Ben, and his lover didn't disappoint, sucking the tender skin hard, marking him for all to see.

"You should have come here with me," Ben growled against his skin.

Tommy nodded and closed his eyes. Yeah, he should have. He'd been trying to prove how independent he was, and instead he'd just insulted the one man in the world he thought might be able to handle him.

Ben's hands found his shirt and he tore at it. The buttons went flying across the room as he ripped it open.

"What the fuck?" Tommy gasped as he looked down at his bare chest, the nipples peaked. What the hell had he done that for? What was he supposed to wear now?

"Now, we're going to say goodnight to our hosts and we're going home so I can remind you exactly who you belong to."

Ben's voice dropped that half octave that made Tommy's knees weaken and his gut churn with desire. He wanted to drop to his knees and worship this man, his submissive side making a bid for some attention. Pushing that aside for the moment when they were home, Tommy swallowed, his cock so hard now that it was trying its best to pop the fly on his jeans.

"Like this?" He indicated his shirt as he asked the question, already knowing the answer. Ben had done that on purpose, a public statement of his ownership.

Ben smiled wickedly, all beautiful white teeth as he un-tucked the rest of Tommy's shirt so it sat a little better on him.

"Oh, yes. I don't want there to be any doubt that you are spoken for. Every man at this party will be clear on the fact that you, my boy, are mine."

Tommy could barely think. "You're fucking serious?"

Could he really do this? Proclaim himself off the market to everyone in that room? Show his body off in that way?

Ben dropped a kiss on his lips and gripped his chin gently.

"I want you, Tommy. I'm putting it out there. If you want me too, come out with me like this and I'll take you home."

Tommy shivered a little, his decision already made. No one made him feel like this man, and he suspected no one else ever would.

He let his hands slide down Ben's hard body until he could cup and stroke Ben's erection through his pants.

"Oh, yeah? And what are we going to do at your place?"

Ben stepped away and held out his hand. "I'm going to fulfill any fantasy you want. Nothing's off limits tonight."

Tommy's knees shook as he took a step forward and slid his fingers into Ben's hand. That was an offer he wasn't going to refuse.

"Let's go then."

Grinning like a fool, Ben opened the door and they stepped out.

Chapter Eight

BEN GRIPPED Tommy's hand and led him out of the safety of the bedroom and into a room full of people. He heard the gasp from his lover and looked back at the way Tommy was hunched over to hide his chest. He wasn't having any of that.

"Stand up straight, handsome. You're not ashamed to be mine, are you?"

Ben did an inward step back. This was the first time his Dom had stepped out of the bedroom, and he couldn't seem to shut him back down. His boy needed a firm hand all right, and he was going to give it to him.

Tommy stared at him for a moment, then straightened up and tossed his head back like a puppet whose strings had been tugged tight.

Ben rewarded him with a kiss on his beautiful mouth, then pulled him through the throng of people. Everywhere men stared, their mouths dropping open comically. Ben just kept moving, not wanting to pay them the smallest bit of attention. Marcus and Danny materialized out of thin air from the kitchen, their eyes wide, smiles huge.

"Ben. Tommy." Marcus nodded at them both as he pulled Danny into his side.

Ben stepped closer to Tommy and wrapped an arm around his neck, sliding his hand down over Tommy's naked breastbone. It was strange, this possessive need he had to dominate Tommy, but his instincts hadn't led him wrong so far, so he was going to continue to follow them.

"We need to get going. Thanks so much for having us."

Tommy's body was stiff, but he raised a hand to Ben's and linked their fingers once again. Triumph filled him.

Marcus cocked an arrogant brow at them. "Maybe you guys could come over for dinner one night this week?"

Ben turned his head so that he was looking at Tommy. "Are we free?"

Tommy nodded and swallowed, his Adam's apple bobbing up and down. "Yeah, though during the week is hard. How 'bout tomorrow night?"

Marcus looked at Danny, who nodded quickly. "Perfect. Seven?"

A surprised laugh burst out of Tommy, vibrations rippling under Ben's hand. "Yeah, seven suits Ben. He's getting old, you know. Can't do the late nights."

Cheeky little shit. Ben pulled his hand back and popped his naughty boy on the ass.

"Ow!" Tommy jumped and turned around with a proper scowl on his face.

Ben laughed and cupped his lover's face, kissing him hard and fast. "Let's go."

Tommy's eyes looked like shimmering pools of blue water, almost transparent in their ability to show Ben exactly what he was feeling.

"Home time, baby."

Tommy put his hand in Ben's, and before long they found themselves in the car, on their way home.

* * *

Ben tugged on Tommy's hand and led him inside, his heart beating like a drum in his chest. The moment he closed the door, he pushed Tommy up against it and grabbed both of his hands. He needed this man so much. Pinning him to the door he dropped kisses over his lover's smooth-shaven cheeks and gorgeous jaw.

"What do you want, baby? Tell me."

No one tasted like Tommy, and Ben was drunk on his flavor. Their lips met, and he thrust his tongue inside, moaning as Tommy sucked on it and ground his hard cock against Ben's.

"Ben..." Tommy moaned and thrust his hips at him.

Ben grunted, dropped his head and bit down on the tender flesh between Tommy's neck and shoulder. "God, you get me so fucking hot."

"Ben, I..."

Ben couldn't tamp down his impatience, and Tommy seemed unable to say more than one word sentences. He bit Tommy's bottom lip, making him gasp with pain.

Moving forward, he put his lips next to Tommy's ear, feeling his lover's shiver. "Tell me, baby. Do you want to fuck me? You can, I'll let you do what no man has ever done to me."

And he would. He'd do anything for this beautiful boy. Tommy groaned and pressed against him harder.

"Or I can dominate the shit out of you, because I believe you need to feel loved, possessed, and wanted."

A feral, desperate noise rose from Tommy's throat. "Yes. Oh, fuck, yes! Please, Ben."

Decision made, Ben pulled back and towed Tommy behind him. They needed a bed, lube, and protection. Fuck, he hated having to use protection with Tommy. He'd never gone bareback before, ever. Had never wanted to. But with Tommy, he didn't want anything between them. He was making the commitment, and he wanted his boy to desire the same kind of relationship he did.

They stepped into his bedroom and he let go of Tommy's hand to find the lube and rubbers, throwing them on the nightstand.

"We're getting tested this week. I don't want to use these things anymore."

Tommy stepped up behind him and pressed his lips to Ben's neck. "Yes, I want that, too."

Ben turned around and admired Tommy, marveling at the beautiful, lean lines of his lover's body.

"You remember your safe word?" A smile pulled up Ben's lips, lightening his mood slightly. He'd never forget that silly word. He hadn't been able to look at a banana and keep a straight face all week.

Tommy nodded, though he trembled. "Yes."

Ben took a step back, his heart thumping so loud he could barely hear above the rush of blood in his ears. "Good. Strip for me."

Tommy pushed his jeans down, revealing no underwear. Ben smiled approvingly.

"Expecting to get lucky tonight, my boy?"

Tommy stepped out of his shoes and threw his clothes across the room. Ben frowned at the mess and pointed to the pile.

"Pick them up and place them on the chair neatly, please. Until you have clothes here, you'll still need to wear them home."

Tommy scowled at him, swaying for a moment in indecision before he stomped over and did as Ben asked, huffing as he went.

Good boy.

"You were about to say?"

Tommy frowned a little more, then walked back to stand in front of Ben. Despite his scowl, he was hard, his erection thrusting proudly up. "Yeah, I was kinda hoping you'd take me home again."

Ben pulled his own shirt off but left his pants on. They'd prevent him from sinking into his boy too soon.

"Then why didn't you message me?" Tommy opened his mouth,

but Ben stopped him with a finger pressed against his lips. "And don't you dare lie to me."

Tommy swallowed and clenched his fists over and over at his sides. "I just wanted to see how I went all week without talking to you. Wanted to see if this feeling would go away."

Ben circled his lover, observing the way Tommy's hard cock bobbed and his muscles shook.

"And what feeling was that, Tommy?"

Tommy dropped his head and flexed his hands together out in front of him. "The ... uh... Damn, I can't explain it."

Ben smacked his boy hard across the ass. "Try."

Tommy jumped and put his hands to his ass, his eyes huge. "The need to have you do everything to me ... all over again."

Still circling his lover, Ben tried hard not to show how pleased he was by Tommy's words. "Just the sex? 'Cuz you know I want more than that."

Tommy shook his head and bit his lip, and the move undid Ben completely. His lover was absolutely adorable. "No, not just the sex. I mean everything."

Ben nodded. That was enough for now. They could talk more after.

"Good. Lie on your belly. Spread-eagled. Arms and legs spread wide."

Ben watched a strange look come over Tommy's face before he nodded and moved over to the bed, lying down a little awkwardly and pushing his hard cock down between his legs.

During the week, Ben had gone to a sex store and had prepared his bed. If this hadn't come to fruition, he would have been mightily pissed off, and more than a little emotionally upset.

He pulled the pillows off the bed, stacking them neatly and revealing the strip of black seatbelt material that was strapped around the mattress, Velcro handcuffs attached.

"What's that?"

Ben chuckled and climbed onto the mattress, straddling Tommy's warm waist.

"I bought us something."

Tommy relaxed beneath him as Ben cuffed his lover's wrists into the Velcro enclosures. "Just for us?"

"Yes," Ben nodded and assured his lover. "Just for us."

He climbed off the bed again and pulled his vibrator out of the bottom drawer, sliding a condom over it. "I've used this on myself, just to see what it would feel like, but I've never used it on anyone else."

Tommy lay still watching him, his face beaded with sweat. "I like that."

Climbing back on the bed, Ben poured some lube down Tommy's ass crack. He gasped and wiggled a little. "That's cold."

Ben smiled to himself. "I've missed this ass, my boy."

He spanked one of Tommy's tight globes and massaged it roughly. The skin flushed and the muscle flexed, while its owner wiggled in his grip.

"Good. It missed you."

Ben caught his chuckle just before it escaped. He loved how much Tommy made him laugh.

Without warning, he slid the lubed vibrator into Tommy's ass, his boy groaning and pressing back wantonly. The vibrator was about half the thickness of his own cock and had a large base, but had other advantages designed to drive his boy to distraction.

"You aren't allowed to come until I say, Tommy."

Moving the vibrator in and out, he watched the way Tommy bucked against it, his wet tipped cock sliding along beneath him.

"What if I can't stop it?"

Ben spanked him hard and thrust the vibrator faster. "You will tell me beforehand so I can change what I'm doing. Trust me. You don't want to push me to punish you."

Ben lowered his voice to increase the threat yet had no idea what he'd do to Tommy if he disobeyed. *Spank him some more? Maybe, though hardly a punishment. Put him in the guest bedroom for the night? No fucking way!*

"Do you understand?"

Tommy moaned and wiggled some more. "Yes."

Ben now wished he'd got a strap for Tommy's ankles too. *Next time.* He turned the vibrator on, and the rotating head began to massage Tommy's prostate. Tommy bucked off the bed, his hips lifting while a scream filled the air.

Ben growled, pushed his lover down and knelt up. "Stop moving."

He slid forward so that his shins were over Tommy's thighs and used his body weight to hold him still, the ass in front of him straining around the vibrator.

"Fuck, Ben! Fuck! Fuck! Fuck!"

Ben turned the speed down and held the vibrator deep. Tommy shuddered. "What, baby? You like this?"

Tommy nodded, his face turned down into the sheets.

"Tell me. Tell me what you like."

"I..."

Ben withdrew the vibrator completely, his heart clenching at the cry of distress Tommy made.

"I fucking like it all, everything you do!" he screamed, still not turning his head.

Ben leaned forward, and lay his body down on Tommy's spine, biting into the flesh of his shoulder. Tommy moaned and turned his head towards him, his sweaty skin pressing up into Ben and making him ache.

"Tell me, baby," Ben repeated, sucking on the skin of Tommy's shoulder until he knew it would bruise.

Tommy huffed and relaxed a little beneath him. "I like you taking control and holding me down."

Ben opened his mouth and bit down hard on the nape of

Tommy's neck. He whimpered softly.

"I like a bit of pain…"

Moving over to the other side of Tommy's neck, Ben bit down, licked and nipped at his flesh.

"I like you wanting me so much."

Ben groaned, flattening himself down so that he could rub his cock on Tommy's back. "I do, baby. God, I do."

"Then fuck me," Tommy begged.

Ben moved back, picked up the vibrator, slid it straight back into Tommy and turned it on high. Tommy's scream filled the bedroom.

"Who do you belong to, Tommy? Who?"

"You!" Tommy's answer was immediate and clear.

"And who gets to fuck this ass?"

"You, Ben!"

Ben pulled the vibrator out, moved back and lifted his boy up onto his shaky knees. His hands trembled as he smoothed a condom down over the weeping head of his cock.

"Anyone else, Tommy? Who else gets to fuck you?"

Tommy pushed back, his arms completely straight as he pulled on his restraints. Ben watched his lover spread his legs to present his balls, tight and pulled up against his body, to Ben's gaze.

"No one! You, only you, Ben! Please!"

Ben set his cock at Tommy's entrance and thrust in, all the way, not stopping to enjoy the tight grip until he was balls deep and Tommy was screaming at him.

"I'm going to come, Ben, please!"

Ben reached under his lover and gave Tommy a few long strokes while he shifted his hips. "Come for me, baby."

Tommy cried out, and wet heat covered Ben's hand. Tommy's body shook and convulsed, his ass squeezing Ben's cock in all the right places. His orgasm teased the base of his spine and he pulled his hand back, straightened up and began to move.

"Tommy, you feel amazing. The best *ever*." He was panting, gripping his lover too hard, and he didn't care. Nothing had ever felt so good.

He pumped into Tommy hard and fast, his lover pushing back against him, moaning out, "More."

Ben saw stars as his thrusts became less measured and his body exploded, cum pouring out of him as pleasure swamped his body, satiation flickering over every nerve cell in his body until he slumped forward, completely drained and sated, over his boy.

Chapter Nine

AFTER THEY HAD COME, Ben had untied him, remade the bed and gently pulled Tommy onto him for a cuddle. He now lay with his head on Ben's chest, still trying to catch his breath. That was the most amazing, incredible sex of his life. If he'd physically been able to come more than once, he would have.

"Thank you, Tommy. That was astounding."

Tommy laughed and moved up so that he was on his back and his head was on a pillow. Ben didn't seem to want to stop touching him and lay a hand on Tommy's chest.

Tommy swallowed and looked his lover straight in the eye. "No, thank you. I've never had anything like that before."

Ben leaned forward and kissed him gently on the mouth, the move strangely cathartic after the possessive passion of their lovemaking. Then he pulled back and looked down at Tommy.

"So, tell me about your life. Why aren't you already taken?"

Tommy picked up the hand Ben had on his stomach and played with his fingers absently.

"Such big hands," he teased as he put his own hand up and saw the way it looked small in comparison.

"The better to touch you with." Ben chuckled and reached down and palmed Tommy's cock.

Tommy arched and closed his eyes, hoping Ben would just continue to touch him. When Ben's hand moved back to his belly, Tommy sighed and opened his eyes.

"What do you want to know, Ben?"

Ben smiled and lifted his hand, tracing his fingertips over Tommy's nose. Feather-light and perfect, it stimulated his very core.

"Tell me why I'm lucky enough to have you. Why didn't some other big idiot snap you up years ago?"

Tommy stared at his lover, turning the question back on him. "Well, why aren't you?"

Ben smiled and ran his talented fingers down Tommy's chest and circled his nipple. "Because I was too busy to even consider anybody, and I'm picky. Very picky."

Lifting his chin, defiant despite everything, Tommy told him, "I'm just the same, Ben."

Ben sighed and rolled onto his back, pulling Tommy with him. Tommy ended up with his head on Ben's chest, listening to his strong, steady heartbeat.

"Baby, I don't want to Dom you all the time. But you need to be honest when you talk to me. It's a pretty simple question."

Now that he wasn't able to look into Ben's eyes from his current position, Tommy found it easier to relax and let the words run free. "I've just never met anyone who wanted me."

"I'm sure plenty of guys wanted you, Tommy." Ben huffed a little and ran a soothing hand up and down his spine. Tommy closed his eyes and savored the way his lover touched him.

Tommy reached up for Ben's nipple, absently playing with the small nub of flesh that hardened instantly. How to make this man understand how new this was for him?

"Yeah, my body maybe. But they didn't care that I had something to say, or they thought I was too hard to handle, or something…" His voice trailed off as he saw the faces of his ex-boyfriends in his mind. The few guys who had stuck around for more than one night.

"No one could see how brilliant you are?" Ben's incredulous tone did wonders to soothe Tommy's battered pride.

"Marcus thought I was clever and hot, but even he didn't stick around for more than a week."

Ben went stiff beneath him, and the hand that was touching Tommy's back halted and flattened against Tommy's spine.

"You've been with Marcus?"

Tommy pushed himself up to look down at Ben's face, anger etched into the lines of his lover's mouth and eyes.

Fuck. Maybe I shouldn't have said anything.

"Yeah, a long time ago."

Ben cupped his face. Tommy turned into the hand that touched him and kissed Ben's palm.

"You know I want you exclusively, right? No other guys while we're together."

Tommy stared at his lover and pressed himself harder into the hands that held him. "It goes both ways, Ben. I'd kill you if you touched anybody else now."

Ben gave him a breathtaking smile and pulled him down for a kiss.

"Good. Now sleep. I haven't slept well all week."

Tommy settled on the thick wall of muscle, hearing the steady, soothing beat of Ben's heart beneath him. "And it's my fault you haven't slept?"

Ben muttered something which Tommy interpreted as, "Yep, completely your fault."

And he smiled, content to close his eyes and let his thoughts wander where they would.

I missed you too.

* * *

Tommy awoke the next morning with a pleasant ache in his ass, and it was increasing.

"Good morning, my beautiful boy." Ben's voice slid into his ear as his finger continued to penetrate his ass.

Tommy arched his back to increase the pressure. "Good morning," he mumbled. Ben added a second finger and pressed deep, pleasure cracking open his skull. "Ah..."

"Roll onto your back, Tommy."

Ben withdrew his fingers, and Tommy winced while he did as his lover had suggested. Ben gave him a soft, slow kiss on his lips before sliding down his body and taking Tommy's cock into his mouth.

Wet heat engulfed the head and he groaned, sliding his hand into Ben's hair. "Ben..."

Ben hummed happily, the vibrations around his cock pure bliss as Ben slid his two fingers back into his sore ass. The ribbon of pain only added to his pleasure, Ben's persistence feeling like possession of the best kind.

"Ow."

Ben moved his mouth faster to distract him, using his hand to stroke his cock and his other fingers rotated around and pressed into his gland. *Ah, yes! Perfect!* Pleasure shot down his legs and he bowed up, his stomach tightening.

"Fuck, Ben, I'm going to come quickly if you keep that up."

Ben twisted his head and stared at Tommy, not releasing his cock for a minute.

He renewed his ministrations, and Tommy hung on to Ben's arm and head while he was swept away on a wave of bliss.

Ben pressed his prostate, sucked the head, and pumped his cock. Tommy was gone.

"Gonna—Ben!"

Ben pressed further down and applied constant pressure. Tommy came so hard he saw stars, his cock pulsing in the most delicious way.

Ben continued to lick him clean until Tommy moaned for him to stop.

"Too sensitive," he sighed as his eyes fluttered shut. Lethargy stole over him.

"Such a good boy. Sleep."

Tommy slipped back under the veil of consciousness, Ben's lips on his forehead.

* * *

Ben made sure Tommy was tucked into bed warmly then awkwardly made his way to the bathroom. He used the toilet, not an easy feat with his cock straining against his belly, then climbed into the shower.

The hot water ran down his back as he licked his lips, the taste of Tommy's seed still lingering there. He grabbed the soap, lubed up his hands and got to work on his own cock.

"Ah, fuck." He moved his hand faster, not interested in making it last.

Tommy got him hard like no man ever had before. His spine began to tingle and his balls pulled up tight as he relived the moment last night he had plunged into his lover.

"Yes..." he hissed out as his knees went weak and his seed flowed out of him.

He tugged the last few drops out of himself and locked his knees to keep from collapsing. *Soap. Focus!* He softly chuckled as he cleaned himself and washed his hair.

He had to train today. It had been days since he'd wanted to. Plus, he couldn't go losing his bulk now. His boy seemed to enjoy it.

He turned off the taps, dried himself and snuck back into his bedroom. He pulled on a pair of grey sweats and a t-shirt, tiptoeing out and letting Tommy sleep a little longer.

He had some paperwork to do, anyway.

* * *

An hour later the man himself stumbled into the study, and Ben's belly gurgled. Perfect timing.

He turned and felt like he'd been punched in the gut. Tommy's hair was all sleep tousled, his blue eyes a little uncertain as he smiled at Ben.

"Hey."

Ben pushed back in his chair and stood up, reaching to pull this beautiful man into his arms.

"Hey. Wanna grab some breakfast?"

Tommy nodded and leaned forward slightly. Ben took the unspoken invitation and pressed his lips to Tommy's, enjoying the way his lover melted into him a little more.

"Let's go." He slung a casual arm around Tommy's shoulders and directed him towards the kitchen. When his lover was propped on one of the barstools by the bench, Ben began pulling food out of the pantry.

"Cereal? Toast? I usually do porridge for myself."

Tommy nodded. "Porridge sounds great. Thanks."

Ben set about making porridge on the stove top, turning away from Tommy to hide his smile. He wanted this every day. He could only hope that Tommy might, too.

"Uh, thanks for my, um ... wake up."

Ben turned and grinned at his lover, stirring the porridge with one hand. "Yeah, well, it was an apology for last night more than anything."

Tommy sat up straighter, his eyes flashing a little. "Apology? Why?"

Ben grinned again. "For going so totally Dom on you. I shouldn't have done that, especially not at Marcus' place. I've never been like that before with anyone."

Tommy shifted on his chair and dropped his eyes. "Don't apologize. I liked it."

Ben focused on stirring, trying hard to not show the surprise he was feeling.

"Good, but I don't want you to stop being you."

Tommy looked up, a cheeky smile flirting with his mouth. "You mean I can go off with whoever I want?"

Ben groaned and lost the battle with himself. "No fucking way."

Tommy smiled some more, his eyes softening. "Then what did you mean?"

"I mean..." What did he mean? "I meant, don't stop being cheeky or bratty. Just because it makes me want to spank you. I don't *need* it, if you hate it."

That was a very risky statement to make. Ben had no idea if he could control his urge to discipline Tommy if it needed to be done. His boy practically begged for it.

Tommy started drawing circles with his fingertips on the marble bench top. "I don't hate it. I like that in you."

Thank God.

"Okay then, good." He turned back to the stove top and turned off the gas. He pulled two bowls down, ladled the porridge, added some honey and placed two spoons into the bowls.

"Let's eat." He walked around to the table and sat down, placing one bowl in front of him and the other opposite him.

Tommy sat down, staring at the porridge as though he hadn't ever seen it before.

"What's wrong?"

Tommy jumped and grabbed the spoon, stirring it to release some of the heat. "Nothing. So, are we really going to Danny and Marcus' for dinner?"

Ben nodded and stirred his own steaming breakfast. "Yeah, of course."

Tommy toyed with his spoon for a bit, then began eating. "As what?" he asked between mouthfuls.

Ah, that's what you want to know.

"Well, exclusive lovers is a bit technical. I'd be happy to go with boyfriend or partner if the topic comes up. Not that Marcus or Danny are going to ask for a title."

Tommy dropped his head, but Ben saw the grin plastered there. "True, but if we met someone on the street, it makes things easier to know what to call you."

Ben's heart rate sped up a little, but he focused on the conversation. "So, you're okay with that?"

Tommy met his eyes once more and nodded.

Ben grinned at him and finished his breakfast. Belly full now, he stretched and moved to the sink.

"I have to get to the gym and supermarket, but do you want to come by here on the way to Marcus'? Or I can pick you up?"

Tommy kissed his neck as he slid the bowl into the sink. "I'll drive here and bring some clothes so that I can go straight to work in the morning."

Ben's breathing hitched, but he ignored it and focused on the dishes. "Okay, cool."

They finished up, and he walked Tommy to his car.

"See you tonight, then."

"Yep." Tommy leaned forward and kissed him, sweet and quick.

Ben headed to the gym, and Tommy headed home. Life was working out pretty fucking good.

Chapter Ten

TOMMY'S DAY PASSED QUICKLY, and he soon found himself climbing the stairs to Marcus' apartment, his hand firmly within Ben's grasp.

Ben smiled at him as he knocked on the door, squeezing his hand reassuringly.

Tommy didn't know why he was so nervous, but he was. This was just Marcus and Danny. He looked over at his lover. *Yeah, and me and Ben.* He shivered, unable to contain the reaction to the new changes in his life. This was big. He had a boyfriend.

The door swung open and Danny stood there, his eyes flickering over their joined hands as he smiled in greeting.

"Hey, guys. So good to see you. Come in."

Danny waved them in, and Ben untangled their fingers. "You first, babe."

Tommy missed the feel of Ben's hand in his immediately. It grounded him somehow.

"Hey, Tommy." Marcus smiled at him as he pulled the cork from a bottle of red. "Thought I'd open up the bottles Ben brought last night."

"Perfect," Tommy murmured as he watched Marcus pour the wine. Ben had brought wine to the party last night? Of course, he had. His boyfriend was a gentleman. The thought made a slightly hysterical smile stretch across his face.

"What's funny?" Ben asked as he slipped a possessive hand around Tommy's waist.

Tommy flinched for a moment, then relaxed against Ben's strength. This public display of affection thing would take some getting used to.

Marcus' smile was a little too big as he poured the wine into four glasses and handed them around their group. "Welcome and cheers."

They clinked glasses and moved into the dining area, sitting at the modern glass table. A buzzer sounded, and Danny hopped up.

"I'll just go check dinner. Back in a minute."

Ben stood up, too. "I'll help you."

Tommy watched his lover's retreating back and sighed. When he turned back to Marcus, his best friend looked as smug as a Cheshire cat.

"What?" he asked, as though he didn't already know.

Marcus shifted forward in his chair and lowered his voice. "Good to see you got back here in one piece. The way Ben was acting last night, I wasn't sure you'd be able to make it tonight."

Tommy smiled and felt his cheeks heat with an embarrassed flush. "Yeah, he's a little possessive sometimes, but it's all good."

Marcus glanced over at the door and tried to move even closer. "So, what happened? Is he into... you know?"

Tommy took another slow sip of his drink and smiled at his friend. Who knew Marcus was so nosy?

"No, I don't know. Is he into what?"

Marcus shifted back and looked embarrassed. "Never mind."

Tommy almost laughed at the petulant look on Marcus's face, but was distracted by the plate Ben placed in front of him. Home-made lasagna, the rich meat sauce and oozing cheese making Tommy's mouth water.

"Yum. Looks great."

Danny put plates down in front of himself, and Marcus and beamed with pride. "Thanks. Mum's recipe."

Danny pushed the salad bowl towards them, and Tommy offered it to his boyfriend. Ben smiled at him "Go for it, babe."

Dropping his eyes to hide his smile, he served himself before handing it over to Ben.

"Thanks for the invite. This is awesome."

Marcus nodded and picked up his utensils. "Dig in."

Tommy ate some of the fresh salad, crunching on the lettuce, tomato, and onion before the smell of the lasagna made him take a bite. "Mmm," he murmured loudly, chewing the perfectly cooked pasta, rich Bolognese sauce, and too much cheese.

"This is really good, Danny," Tommy said between mouthfuls as everyone at the table agreed with resounding nods and murmuring as they ate quickly.

It was just too good to slow down.

"I'm so going to get fat," Tommy complained as he rubbed his belly happily.

Ben laughed and poked him. "Yeah, right. And it'd be good if you did a little, so then everywhere we go the men would stop drooling over you."

Tommy felt his mouth drop open a little. Then he picked up his wine and buried his smile in his drink. Ben wasn't afraid to say those sorts of things in company, and how good was that?

"My compliments to the chef." Ben beamed at Danny, placing his arm along the back of Tommy's chair while rubbing his stomach with his other hand.

"Well, I have to do something while Marcus works all day." Danny rolled his eyes at his boyfriend, and Marcus shrugged.

"What? I can't help it if my projects can't be finished during office hours."

Then Marcus launched into a detailed conversation about his current project, and Tommy let his mind wander.

Wonder what Ben will think of to do tonight? I haven't done anything to annoy him yet, but maybe I could just pretend to be bad and we could roleplay. He might like that.

Ben's hand shaking his shoulder brought him back to the conversation.

"Huh, sorry?"

"Baby, what are you working on at the moment?"

Tommy turned his head and stared at his lover. No one had ever asked about his work. Come to think of it, he couldn't remember the last time anyone other than a client had asked him a question and actually cared what came out of his mouth.

"Ah, nothing special."

Marcus opened his mouth to keep the conversation going, but Ben cleared his throat loudly and turned in his chair to face him.

"No, seriously, babe. Tell me. I want to know."

Tommy swallowed hard and began to explain about the shopping center extension he had begun to design. Ben asked questions, and Danny seemed interested too. *Amazing.*

Before Tommy knew it, it was time to leave and they headed for the door.

"Thank you so much. We had a great time."

Danny smiled and waved at them as they walked out the door. "At least your shirt is still in one piece tonight, Tommy."

Tommy laughed but glared playfully at his friends. It was all in good fun.

"Not for long," Ben told them as he waved his goodbye.

Ben took his hand and pulled him down the stairs, Marcus and Danny's cackling laughter following them down the entire three flights down to the parking lot.

"Why'd you say that?" Tommy asked and was soon turned around and pressed against Ben's car.

"Because it's true. When we get home, I'm going to rip this shirt off you and make you scream."

Tommy swallowed the lump in his throat as he looked up at his big teddy bear.

"Thank you for tonight." He slipped his arms around Ben and his lover's face softened instantly, his aggressive mood forgotten.

"What for? I had a great time too."

Tommy kissed Ben's thick, beautiful lips and forced himself to get it out. "I want you to know I appreciate all of it. Everything. You being affectionate, and encouraging me to talk. I feel ... special with you around."

Ben chuckled and pressed his forehead to Tommy's, the warmth sinking through to heat all the neglected, cold corners of his soul.

"Tommy, you *are* special in every way. It's my job to make you feel that way each day."

Tommy enjoyed the moment for a second more before he moved his head and eyed his lover. "Really? Because my ass is unimpressed."

"Huh?" Ben's mouth hung open comically, and Tommy forced his eyebrows to remain stern and not laugh.

"I looked in the mirror this morning, and there wasn't a mark on me. How am I supposed to get through every day without that physical reminder of you?"

Ben literally growled and swooped down for a kiss, his lips possessive with his passion. His tongue stole into Tommy's mouth, and he closed his eyes.

Epilogue

HAPPILY EVER AFTER

"YOU KNOW HE PROPOSED IN *PARIS*?" Tommy rolled his eyes at the soppy move his best friend had pulled. He leaned harder against the wall of muscle that was his hunky man, Ben.

"Yeah, so?" Ben licked his earlobe, the heated wetness making him shiver as the autumn breeze blew around them.

"Stop, I can't concentrate."

It may have been a bit over the top, even for Marcus, but he couldn't deny how happy they looked.

Danny held Marcus' hands and was staring at him like a puppy dog.

Marcus, Tommy's best friend since university days, cleared his throat and smiled at his toy boy.

"Danny, I love you. You are everything that is good and pure in this world. You make me laugh, you make me cry, and you give me a peace that I didn't know existed. Today I pledge to always love you, stand by you, and support you in everything that we do in this life."

Wow.

Despite himself, Tommy felt hot prickling at the back of his eyes, and he dug his fingernails into his palms to force the tears away.

"You can't be jealous. Seriously?" Ben's voice had a hard note to it that made a cool shiver pass over Tommy's body.

He looked up at his lover, noticing the tense angle of his jaw and the slight hurt in his eyes. That wouldn't do. Ben was the best partner any man had ever had.

He relaxed his posture to lean into Ben a little more, stroking his lover's arm in a bid to reassure him.

"No, of course not. It's just... I mean, look at them. I didn't expect to like this so much."

Danny grinned up at Marcus and began his own sappy speech.

"Marcus, you're the best man I've ever met. I admire you, respect you, and most of all, I love you. You've given me everything I've ever wanted, and today you give me a dream I dared not have."

He leaned up to whisper into Ben's ear. "That's true. What gay guy honestly dreamt of white silk bows and a wedding at an expensive reception center?"

Ben chuckled and poked him, both of them looking back at the celebrant.

"I now pronounce you life partners. You may kiss your husband."

Tommy watched the two lock lips for the thousandth time. They never stopped pashing, those two, not that he was any better. If Ben wasn't kissing him, he was touching him in some way. Always.

Case in point, he looked down to his hip where Ben's possessive hand rested. He had everything he had ever wanted, too. A man who loved him and fucked him within an inch of his life on a regular basis. What else was there?

A general cry arose around them, and he straightened up to clap as everyone stood and stepped forward to congratulate the newly married couple.

Seriously, why would Marcus want to get hitched? It was one of the main advantages to being gay! You didn't need to put up with some whiny woman who wanted to get married.

"Let's get something to eat, baby. We can congratulate them later."

Ben took his hand and pulled him away from the garden wedding. They were at a nice little reception center, and Tommy couldn't wait for the food.

"When do we eat?"

Ben laughed and tugged him into the reception room filled with white tables and chairs decorated with silver bows. Tommy could smell the roast lamb and rosemary, and his mouth watered at the scent.

"Later. I want to show you something first."

Ben tugged hard and fell forward as they entered a small room, richly decorated and containing half empty trays of drinks.

"This where they got ready, do you think?"

"Hmmm." Ben made an agreeing, humming noise and came up behind him.

Hot, strong arms enfolded him, and Tommy's eyes slid shut.

No way.

"You want to..."

He gasped as Ben bit into his neck, the sharp prickles and heat making him moan as arousal pulsed through him. Ben's hand moved over him, cupping his hardening cock through his suit pants and flicking his pierced nipples through his shirt.

"Yes. I want you."

Ben unbuckled Tommy's belt with fast, efficient movements, the material of his suit pants sliding down his legs and falling to the floor within moments.

He wore no underwear, as Ben liked him commando. He groaned as cool air circled his hot balls and Ben's strong hands pressed between his shoulder blades, forcing him forward. He reached out for the table in front of him, the wood solid beneath his hands.

"You sure we've..."

Ben spanked his butt, and the sting made him gasp as the sound ricocheted around the room. He dropped his head, letting the feelings of love and trust flow through him. He shouldn't be asking. Ben had never disappointed him, ever. He'd also never let them get caught, and they'd fucked in more weird places than Tommy had ever dreamed of.

Ben's strong, warm hands ran over the flesh of his ass and thighs, making his skin tingle and his body ache for so much more. He opened his legs as wide as he could with his pants around his ankles, hoping the not so subtle hint would get him what he needed.

Ben's warm lips traced a path across his buttocks as he reached around and wrapped his hand around Tommy's semi hard cock, stroking it in sure, smooth movements.

"Oh, fuck! Ben..."

Heat whirled around him as Ben's free hand pulled his hip further back so he was poking his ass out and Ben's tongue ran a line down his crack.

God, he is so good at that.

Ben's tongue pressed against his hole, and Tommy pushed his hips back, wanting the invasion as much as his next breath.

Ben let go of Tommy's cock and pressed forward, breaching his hole with his tongue while holding his cheeks open with his strong, big hands. Pleasure burst through Tommy's balls, and he let out a feral sound.

"Ah..." Tommy let his eyes close and moaned in time with the thrusting of Ben's tongue, his cock throbbing in time with Ben's talented movements.

His balls began to tighten, and his belly clenched as he got more and more excited.

The heat and pressure were gone, and he groaned in sweet frustration.

"You didn't think it would be that easy, beautiful boy?"

Ben's voice had deepened to a level that sent goose bumps all over Tommy's flesh. That was the sound of his lover in heat, and he knew that would mean an amazing session for both of them.

Tommy shook his head *no* and shuffled his feet to turn around, watching as his lover undid his belt and zipper and took out his hardening cock.

"Help me with this, would you?" Ben asked with a cheeky smile, and Tommy dropped to his knees on the plush carpet, engulfing as much of the hot, hard flesh as he could.

Ben's hand wrapped around his skull with the perfect amount of pressure, encouraging him to move in a rhythm as natural as breathing. Tommy smiled and hummed as he moved up and down on Ben's cock. He loved the groans and gasps his lover made, the air around them heating up with their combined lust and need to love.

He swirled his tongue around the large head and sucked hard, tasting the salty pre-cum that seeped from the small slit.

"Enough." Ben pulled him off, tugged him up and spun him around in sharp, fast movements.

Tommy's breath came in pants, his heart beating against his chest as he grinned and wiggled his hips, loving the power that was now pulsing through him. Ben needed him as much as Tommy needed his big bear. That always gave him a great sense of security.

Foil ripped and hot hands caressed his naked hips, making him bite his lip and grip the desk hard. They didn't use protection much anymore, but considering he had to sit in a suit for the next five hours, Tommy appreciated the attempt at neatness.

Lube-slick fingers pressed against him, then breached his body with slow, sure skill.

He hissed as the pain spread through him and gasped as Ben's finger swept inside him, pressing against the sweet spot.

Tommy slowed his breathing and concentrated on relaxing his muscles, moaning in relief when the pain blended and disappeared as the pleasure rose. Ben added another finger, scissoring them and stretching him.

"You want me, sweetheart?" Ben's hand caressed his lower back and pressed deeper inside him.

Tommy opened his legs as wide as he could. This wasn't the time to play coy.

"You know I do."

Ben's fingers withdrew and latex pressed against him, Ben's thick cock teasing his ass.

Tommy flexed his hips and tried to get Ben's cock inside him.

His lover hissed, then laughed.

"Cheeky little shit."

Tommy grinned and Ben slid home, filling him up and stretching him further than he thought was possible.

"Oh God."

"Fuck, you feel divine, Tommy."

Tommy grunted, pleasure flowing over his body like a hot shower. All encompassing, powerful, and so strong, he couldn't talk or think.

"I've never wanted anyone the way I want you. You drive me ... out of ... my mind." Ben could still speak, obviously. He moved back, then slid home again, starting a rhythm designed to drive them both over the edge.

Tommy moved with the thrusts and slid his hand to his hip, linking his fingers with his lovers', humming when Ben gripped tight, sealing their connection.

"You are the best thing that's ever happened to me. You know that?"

Ben grunted as he began to move faster and harder, his hips punctuating the air around them with the sound of their skin slapping together.

Tommy heard Ben's words and nodded blindly. His orgasm was gathering again, and he'd struggle to stop it this time.

Ben began to hiss, his breathing changing to a pant. He was close, too.

Thank God for that.

Tommy squeezed his ass around Ben's cock, gasping as Ben thrust hard, burying himself to the hilt.

Ben's hand snaked around Tommy's hip, slick with lube, and pumped on his cock.

Tommy cried out as he lost the battle to hold on to his orgasm. Fire licked at his balls, and he groaned, his cum boiling up inside him and spurting out in hot pulsing waves.

"Oh, fuck." He gasped and moaned as Ben moved gently, pegging his prostate perfectly to lengthen his pleasure.

The fireworks going off in his head began to disappear and his hearing returned just in time to hear Ben groan out his own release, his hands squeezing tight on Tommy's hips.

"Wow." Tommy blinked several times, rolling his head to the side as Ben leaned forward and pressed a kiss to his neck.

"I love you." Ben's words floated across his skin, and Tommy smiled to himself, relaxing his whole body.

"I love you, too." It was so easy to say the words now.

His lover slipped his now softening cock out, and Tommy sighed, the twinge of strange pain making him ache for Ben to be back inside him.

Tommy cleaned himself quickly with some nearby tissues and pulled his pants back up. He did up his fly and belt, his head swimming with lethargy and stars.

He turned to watch Ben, already cleaned up, drop onto a nearby chaise lounge, looking all sexy and way too beautiful.

"Well, don't you look all old-fashioned and shit."

Tommy swallowed as Ben pinned him with a glare, his eyebrows lowered and his eyes hard. "That good, was it?"

Tommy inhaled sharply through his nose and bit his lip. Ben knew him too well.

"Yeah, it was. You're an incredible lover, Ben."

"Look who's talking."

"What are we doing now, babe?"

Ben patted the chaise and gave him a slow smile. "Come sit for a minute, and then we'll go join the party."

Tommy loped towards his partner, an unease creeping into his belly.

"Something wrong?"

Ben shook his head and reached out, touching Tommy's hand and pulling him down onto the lounge with a strong tug.

Soft lips touched his before Ben pivoted and dropped to the floor on one knee.

"What the hell are you doing?"

Ben grinned up at him and pulled out a small black box.

Oh, hell no!

"Fuck no, Ben! I'm not some damn chick you can..." Tommy went to stand up, and his big bear grabbed his arms and pulled him back down hard, his ass landed on the leather seat with a small slap.

"Sit down, baby boy, and shut up." Ben's tone was harsh and no nonsense. It calmed Tommy immediately, and he took a better look at the man who was now not only his lover, but his best mate, too.

His brown eyes were hard, but there was an insecurity there that made Tommy sit up straighter.

"What's this about, babe?"

Ben huffed and gripped Tommy's thigh with his free hand.

"This is about us, and how much I love you. I know you don't believe in any of this crap, but I do. I want the world to know you're mine, that we're committed to each other."

Tears began to gather at the back of Tommy's eyes, making them prickle and burn.

Ben continued, "You're the most important thing in the world to me. I want you to marry me, bond with me, whatever the hell you want to call it, but I want to have a party and stand up in front of all our friends and commit to a life together. Can you do that with me?"

Tommy blinked several times, his stomach jumping with excited elephants.

"You really want to do all that?" Tommy waved in the direction of the door, and the people outside it in the reception hall.

Ben squeezed his thigh and nodded once. "Yes, but it doesn't have to be like this. It can be on a beach, or our house. It can be a hundred friends or just our family. I don't care, whatever you want. But I want to show you and the rest of the world how much I love you."

Well, if that wasn't one of the best bloody speeches he'd ever heard.

"I think you just wrote your vows there. That's pretty impressive."

Ben's eyes went wide.

"Is that a yes?"

Tommy grabbed Ben's beloved face with both hands and gave him the only answer that was possible. "Of course, it is! I adore you, you big, beautiful man!"

Ben dove forward, their lips connecting with a passion and heat that made Tommy run his hands around Ben's head and grip his skull, wanting him to stay there forever.

Their tongues mated and caressed. Then the kiss changed, Ben slowing everything down and softly kissing him.

Ben pulled back and rubbed his nose against Tommy's, the simple gesture enough to make Tommy's eyes sting once again.

He'd never thought he'd love anyone the way he loved Ben.

"Ben ... I..." His voice cracked, and he coughed to clear his throat.

His lover gave him an understanding grin, got to his feet and stepped away.

"Let's go, gorgeous. We've got a reception to attend."

Tommy stood up and moved forward, part of him feeling drunk or surreal. Had he just agreed to *marry* Ben? Who would have thought it was possible? Ben unlocked the huge wooden door and opened it for Tommy to walk through.

Tommy grinned at his man. "Well, thank you."

Ben chuckled and slapped Tommy on the ass as he walked past, the tingles ricocheting through to his belly.

"Let's go."

Ben slipped his hand into Tommy's palm, the heat and strength making him flush with pleasure. He found Ben's need to be affectionate in public flattering, but also a little embarrassing.

Tommy glanced around him, wondering if anyone was watching them. But all he saw were a whole group of men and women milling around tables and chairs.

"We're at table two, gorgeous." Ben's silky voice caressed his neck, and Tommy chuckled as he veered that way and tugged Ben along behind him.

He settled in his chair and looked around the room. Flowers, white silk, and cheesy candle crap everywhere.

"Our wedding is *not* going to be like this!"

Ben laughed and sat in the chair next to him, his hand sliding onto Tommy's thigh in that possessive way he had.

"I told you, you can have whatever you like."

Tommy hummed and reached for his bread roll, ripping it apart and munching down on the soft white carb that once upon a time he wouldn't have gone anywhere near.

"Everyone, please take a seat. The entrées are about to be served." Marcus' smooth voice filled the room, and people took their places with speedy efficiency.

"Technically, we have speeches a little bit later, but I am hoping to make one quick announcement before we all start eating."

Marcus' eyes zoomed in on them, and Tommy looked at Ben.

"Is he looking at us for a reason?"

Ben swallowed and nodded at Marcus. "Yeah, he is. Stand up."

Tommy moved to his feet, his cheeks flushing with heat as all one hundred sets of eyes turned on them.

Ben's arm stole around him, pulling him in tight.

He seemed to nod again, and Marcus chuckled into the microphone.

"Tommy has been my best friend for over ten years, and I want to be the first to congratulate him on his engagement. It seems that Ben is finally going to make an honest man of the one blond many said would never be tamed."

No fucking way! Ben, I'm going to kill you.

A loud roar went up, and Tommy turned into Ben, his lover's hands holding him close.

"You prick," he whispered against Ben's shirt, turning back towards the crowd, knowing that hiding now would be stupid.

Ben grabbed his hands and turned him back again, staring down at him with intense eyes.

"I want the world to know you're mine, Tommy, and you are surrounded by people who love you. You always will be."

Tommy glanced towards the stage and saw Danny stand up and clap, smiling from ear to ear.

He looked back at Ben and leaned in, moaning as Ben's lips parted and his tongue swept into Tommy's mouth.

Fuck propriety.

Tommy grabbed on to Ben's shirt and hauled him closer, spearing his tongue back into Ben's mouth.

He wasn't just Ben's, the big bear was *his*. Always and forever.